STOP THOSE MONSTERS!

STOP

For Tobey and Amy, always
- Steve Cole

For Steph, Denis and Jasper
- Jim Field

OTHER STORIES BY STEVE COLE:

MAGIC INK ☙ ALIENS STINK
ASTROSAURS ☙ COWS IN ACTION ☙ SLIME SQUAD
TRIPWIRE ☙ YOUNG BOND

A MAGIC INK PRODUCTION ☙ FIRST PUBLISHED IN GREAT BRITAIN IN 2015 BY SIMON AND SCHUSTER UK LTD ☙ A CBS COMPANY ☙ TEXT COPYRIGHT © STEVE COLE 2015 ILLUSTRATIONS COPYRIGHT © JIM FIELD 2015 ☙ THIS BOOK IS COPYRIGHT UNDER THE BERNE CONVENTION ☙ NO REPRODUCTION WITHOUT PERMISSION ☙ ALL RIGHTS RESERVED THE RIGHT OF STEVE COLE AND JIM FIELD TO BE IDENTIFIED AS THE AUTHOR AND ILLUSTRATOR OF THIS WORK RESPECTIVELY HAS BEEN ASSERTED BY THEM IN ACCORDANCE WITH SECTIONS 77 AND 78 OF THE COPYRIGHT, DESIGNS AND PATENTS ACT, 1988. ☙ 10 9 8 7 6 5 4 3 2 1 SIMON & SCHUSTER UK LTD ☙ 1ST FLOOR, 222 GRAY'S INN ROAD, LONDON WC1X 8HB ☙ WWW.SIMONANDSCHUSTER.CO.UK ☙ SIMON & SCHUSTER AUSTRALIA, SYDNEY SIMON & SCHUSTER INDIA, NEW DELHI WWW.MAGICINKPRODUCTIONS.COM A CIP CATALOGUE RECORD FOR THIS BOOK IS AVAILABLE FROM THE BRITISH LIBRARY. PB ISBN: 978-0-85707-874-2 ☙ EBOOK ISBN: 978-0-85707-875-9 THIS BOOK IS A WORK OF FICTION. NAMES, CHARACTERS, PLACES AND INCIDENTS ARE EITHER THE PRODUCT OF THE AUTHOR'S IMAGINATION OR ARE USED FICTITIOUSLY. ANY RESEMBLANCE TO ACTUAL PEOPLE LIVING OR DEAD, EVENTS OR LOCALES IS ENTIRELY COINCIDENTAL. PRINTED AND BOUND BY CPI GROUP (UK) LTD, CROYDON, CRO 4YY

THOSE MONSTERS!

STEVE COLE

ILLUSTRATED BY JIM FIELD

CHAPTER 0

A NOTE FROM  PRODUCTIONS

Long ago, when people were apes, elephants were mammoths, tigers came with sabre-teeth and monkeys were smaller, fatter and a bit squirrelly . . .

The first monsters appeared on the Earth.

They squelched across every continent.

They lurked in every sea.

They evolved just like everything else.

They made guest appearances in many myths and legends (and were usually the best thing about them).

Only . . . see any monsters about you now?

No. No, you don't.

WHERE DID ALL THE MONSTERS GO?

You are about to find out.

For the monsters have a world of their own: a world of mysteries without measure and dangers without end. A world that few have visited, and fewer still survived to tell the tale. Or indeed any tale at all, apart from a very short and uninspiring tale that sounds suspiciously like:

AUUGGHHH HHHHHHHH!

This book goes further than any other to bring you, for the first time, the

VHOLE, REVOLTING TRUTH.

So STRAP YOURSELF IN – it's going to get

MONSTERY . . .

CHAPTER 1

HELP! MY HOUSE HAS BEEN KIDNAPPED!

Er, sorry, I know you've just started reading this book and everything, but this isn't really the easiest time for me to write.

My house has just been picked up by some crazy, freaky hurricane. Right now it's being whirled about the sky like a giant's conker, and I'm in the wardrobe, just trying to hang on.

Well, anyway, just look at the state of my room! All my DVDs thrown all over the place . . . tops, trousers and dirty pants everywhere . . . books and collectibles

1

scattered over the floor (and on the bed) . . . okay, so my room normally looks like this anyway. In fact, my mum would probably be more freaked out that I haven't tidied up yet than by the fact our house is hurtling through a hurricane, and — unless we had some really paranoid builders on this estate — no massive rocket jets underneath to help us safely land again.

*ROCKETS NOT INCLUDED

So, basically. Noooooooooo, we're gonna crash down *on the other side of town, and everything including me will be smashed to pieces and I really don't wanna think about that—*

It's probably a good job Mum is out with my dad for dinner tonight. Though I'm not sure Rachel Thing saw it that way (I can't remember her proper surname.) Rachel Thing is the babysitter who was downstairs; I think she jumped ship (or house) not long after we took off into the air. I definitely heard her yell and the front door open, and after that . . . nothing. She's only in Year Ten while I'm in Year Eight, so I'm not sure she's even qualified to babysit. She might be qualified in skydiving out of low-flying houses, though.

I should have jumped too, before the house was so high. But I was so scared, I couldn't move. I couldn't even shout for help. And now I'm wishing I collected airline sick-bags instead of monster movie memorabilia. Empty sick-bags, obviously (who collects full ones? Weird!). Because if the house keeps on rollercoastering through the clouds like this, I'm going to start redecorating my room in shades of Technicolor vomit. And that's going to ruin my cool collection of vintage horror-film posters. If only I'd got them framed like Dad told me to, instead of using Blu-Tack, they'd just wipe clean!

Ooops, but there goes my bedside table, right into The Wolf Man's teeth, so if they had been framed, the glass would've shattered and the air filled with lethal shards and everything would be at least 28% worse.

Blue sky and green fields flip past the bedroom window, but there's a yellow glow, too, and it's getting brighter.

The room is shaking like a space shuttle attempting re-entry. The turbulence turns my stomach like the world's worst waltzer.

Then – **WHAMMMMMM!**

It's like my eyes are struck by lightning. I'm thrown out of the wardrobe and bang my head against the radiator.

"OWWWWWWW!" I yell. Sound from my throat, at last! I follow up the "OWWWWWWW" with some random shouting and cursing – it takes my mind off throwing up.

And so does the view through my window.

Because suddenly there's no blue sky, no fields, no random flying animals caught up in the storm. There's not even a yellow glow any more. There's only darkness, rolling and roiling like the inside of a thundercloud.

And then – "WHOOAAAAAAAAAA!!!!!" – the whole house tips over and I'm thrown against the window, and it opens and . . .

I'm falling through darkness. It's what you might call a 'brown trousers' moment. (Doubly so, as I actually AM wearing brown trousers. What were the chances?!)

I glimpse my house spinning away into shadows beneath me.

On and on, I fall. Tiny. Insignificant. Doing little fearful farts as I go. (You totally can't blame me.) But I can smell something worse than those little butt-whimpers. Something rotten and rancid and all kinds of wrong—

And suddenly, I crash into it.

CHAPTER 2

THE SKY IS MADE OF MUD!

I woke up upside down in a tree.

It was a weird tree. It was white. Not like a silver birch, more like the unhealthy white of something that's never seen any sun. Maggot white. And the leaves! They were furry – like big, squashed caterpillars. And the branches weren't hard, they were spongy. Dozens of twigs hooked out from every squishy branch like creepy crab-legs. And it smelled disgusting, rotten; like something had died here.

Please, don't let the dead thing be me, I thought. *And please don't let it be Rachel the babysitter. That would be super gross.*

But no, she *must've* got out – I heard the front door. She

totally left me to die! Or to fall into a tree, anyway. Just let her try claiming £7 an hour from Mum and Dad after this . . .

My brain felt scrambled. My senses felt fried. Was a part of me poached or hard-boiled? I didn't want to know. I closed my eyes, hoping everything would look better when I opened them again.

It didn't. I was still lying upside down in a maggot-white, squashed-caterpillary, spongy, crab-leggy tree.

Barely daring to move in case anything had broken in the fall, I craned my (apparently unbroken) neck to see what I could see. The tree was standing in a park of pink grass. You know those fake tinselly Christmas trees you get cheap from B&Q? The grass was kind of like that. It looked like foil.

Beyond the fake grass was a brown, muddy, car-less road, and on the other side of that was a row of funny, crooked houses made of yellow bricks.

The houses seemed to stretch as far as the eye could see in both directions. They were the same basic design, although weirdly, the doors were different shapes and sizes. I caught glimpses of movement through the windows. Curtains were twitching.

"What's the matter," I muttered, "never seen a boy hanging upside down in a freaky tree that smells like death?"

I raised my head towards my feet. At least the sun was shining, after that terrible darkness I'd fallen through . . .

I froze.

How could you have frozen? I hear you cry. *You just said the sun was shining!*

Yes, I did say that. Because I thought it was true.

But I was wrong.

It wasn't the sun that was shining. It was a ma-hoosive light bulb, dangling down from the sky. Well, I say 'sky'. I mean 'roof'.

The sky was made of mud. Seriously. I stared at it for ages and ages, just to make sure. A roof of solid dirt stretched overhead for as far as I could see. Roots dangled down here and there, and other light bulbs hung from sockets in the soil.

"That settles it," I said calmly. "I have sooooooo got to be asleep. How can I possibly be underground?" I'd watched a creaky old sci-fi movie called *Things to Come* on BluRay the other day, where future humans end up living in big underground cities. That must be it! I was dreaming and the idea must've sneaked into my dream.

Phew.

I tried to pinch myself awake, but nothing changed. Maybe I was in a really deep sleep?

Or ... perhaps it was more serious than that? "Perhaps," I breathed, "when I fell, I bumped my hea— ADDDDDDDD!"

I fell out of the tree and bumped my head. And as I struck that spongy, unnaturally-tinselly ground, I heard a great gasp of surprise go up from the edge of the park.

Dizzily, I looked round – and did a pretty good gasp of my own. While I'd been staring at the light bulb in the sky, different-sized locals had crept out of the different-sized doors in their houses, crowding together to watch me.

I say 'locals'.

I mean

MONSTERS.

CHAPTER 3

WHAT'S A GIANT HAMSTER IN A TOGA LIKE YOU DOING IN A PLACE LIKE THIS? OH, HANG ON, NO, THIS IS EXACTLY THE PLACE I'D EXPECT TO FIND A GIANT HAMSTER IN A TOGA. SORRY!

I couldn't believe what I was seeing. THINGS, of all shapes and colours. At least thirty of them. Some had huge, boggly eyes, others had little squinty peepers on stalks. Some had mouths full of teeth, and some had only green gums to gnash together. And I knew – I just knew – that these weren't people dressed up, or animatronics, or CGI projections.

The monsters were REAL.

Now, this might sound strange to you, but for a few moments I wasn't afraid. Not properly afraid. I felt maybe 32% afraid, but around 36% excited and 32% full of wonder. See, I've always loved the idea of real-life monsters. I was never scared of creepy creatures under the bed. In fact, I used to leave out milk and biscuits to entice them into my room. I used to sleep under the bed sometimes, in the hope I'd find one there.

I even wrote letters to the Tooth Furry — no fairies for me, thanks — in the hope I'd wake up to find a small flying monster, covered in fluff, wrestling with my manky molars.

I know all kids are supposed to do cute, quirky stuff like this. My mum said it was because I wanted to be like my grandad, who got me into creaky old monster movies in the first place. He used to stay up late to watch them, like, a hundred years ago, with his dad — in the days of black-and-white portable TVs, when there were only about two channels and you could only get a picture by turning a dial and sticking a wire coathanger in the back, etc etc. (Have you heard adults spout this sob story like it's our fault we were born in the age of HD on demand? Deal with it, guys.)

Anyway, I lay there in a daze, still kind of expecting to wake up in my home (wherever the flip it was now). And I reached out a hand in a way I hoped looked friendly and unthreatening, and said: "Hey . . . !"

AUUUGHHHHHHHH!!!

It was a total monster stampede. It was like I was the scary one, getting up from the weird, pink grass on my wobbly legs. As the dust cloud cleared I saw that just one monster had stayed behind.

For a moment I wasn't sure it really counted as a monster – it looked more like someone had inflated a hamster to the size of a sheepdog, dressed it in a grubby toga and taught it to walk on its back legs. It was plump and fluffy, with bright black eyes open as wide as its mouth as it stared at me.

"Hey!" squeaked the hamster thing. "I'm Verity. How you doing?"

"Uh . . . me?" I looked cautiously behind me in case the giant hamster (called Verity?!) was talking to someone else. "I'm . . . Well, I'm . . ."

"Human!" Verity clutched her little paws together and smiled, showing big, beavery buckteeth. "You are, aren't you? A human being? An ACTUAL HUMAN BEING!"

"Um, yes," I agreed.

"I'VE FOUND ONE!" she squealed, and bundled towards me. "AT LAAAAAAAST!"

"Wha—!" If I'd actually needed proof that this monster was real, rather than some sort of giant hologram, I got it there and then. As Verity clutched me clumsily to her I felt her heart pounding through her musty toga, spluttered on a mouthful of fur, was scratched by a whisker and felt the rasp of her tongue as she gave me a lick on the face.

"URPHHH!"

"Oooooh!" Verity suddenly broke off her hug attack and gazed at me, entranced. "Tell me, human, what is this human thing called 'Urphhh?' Is it your name?"

"No! My name's Bob."

"Bob-ob-ob," she repeated in a low voice. "Bobobob. Bob-Bob-Bob. BOB-B-B-B-B-"

"And I went 'Urphhh' because you . . . well, you . . ." I suddenly noticed just how big and sharp those teeth of hers were. "Er . . . no reason."

"Are you normal, Bob-ob-ob?" Verity asked eagerly, doing a sort of stutter on the last 'b'. "Are you, Bob-ob-ob? Are you?"

"Um, it's just 'Bob'—"

"See, I've always dreamed of spotting a NORMAL human being, Bob-ob-ob. I never knew they could find

17

their way down here to Terra Monstra."

"To where?"

"Terra Monstra. Or, **MONSTERLAND**, to you!" Verity gave me a wink. "But, you know, monsters, schmonsters, Bob-ob-ob. Who cares? There's thousands of 'em down here."

My mouth felt dry. "Thousands?"

"Yeah, monsters galore. But no humans! Humans live way up topside. They're super-ultra-rare! That's why that bunch of cowards ran away from you."

I was kind of glad they had. "What were they scared of?"

"Well, **YOU**, I guess," Verity said brightly. "See, they know all the old stories about humans. They think that any minute now you will start a war, or pollute the environment, or make a species extinct, or start an evil bank that will cripple the monster economy . . ."

"I wouldn't do that!" I spluttered. "Humans do good stuff too."

Verity winked. "Ah, you say that, but . . ."

"They must do!" I tried to think of something but my mind was blank. "Anyway . . ." I eyed her warily. "You don't seem very scared of me."

"I'm not! I understand you better, see? Cos I'm a human spotter!" Verity couldn't stop herself from giving me another lick on the face. "Yum! Cheek of Bob-ob-ob!"

"Eww!" I cringed, and took a step backwards, afraid she'd get a taste for it. "What do you mean, a human spotter?"

"I mean," she said slowly, as if I was thick, "I spot humans up topside through my uncle's humanoscope! Uncle Voshto built it to peer into your funny human world. He used to be Professor of Humanology at Disgusting University down on Level Two. When I grow up I want to be just like him. He knows **EVERYTHING** about humans. Not like those scaredy-blaggle monsters over there." She turned to the row of houses. "It's all right, scaredy-blaggles! This human is a boy human! He's a bit stupid but he means well!"

There was no movement from the houses, just the odd twitching curtain. Here I was, alone in an unknown world of monsters, and THEY were afraid?

"What a cheek!" I said.

"Mmm, yes." Verity licked my face again. "Cheek of Bob-ob-ob! It's deelish…!"

But I was barely listening any longer. I guess the shock of my fall and the hurricane and all that was wearing off, and panic was gearing up to take its place. Suddenly my head was crowding with questions, a whole load of them, ready to burst . . .

How did I get here?

How can you exist, weirdo hamster-thing called Verity?

WHAT IF ALL THE MOVIE MONSTERS I'VE EVER SEEN ARE REAL AND LIVE DOWN HERE?

Am I still dreaming?

ARE YOU SAYING HUMANOLOGY IS A THING HERE?

What kind of a freaky tree is that?

What is a humanoscope?

What the flipping
flippety-flip is going on?

Have I gone super-bonkers nuts-loopy?

*SERIOUSLY,
ARE WE UNDERNEATH
THE REAL WORLD?*

WHERE HAS MY HOUSE GONE?

HOW DO I GET BACK?

HOW DO I GET BACK?!

HOW DO I
GET BACK?!!!

Luckily, before I could fully switch to 'flap about like a looper pretending to be a teapot' mode, the sound of a siren brought me back to Earth (or under it, anyway).

It's the police! I thought hopefully, as the screeching siren grew louder, closer. *They've come to rescue me!*

But, no.

It wasn't the police.

A massive vehicle – heavy, armoured and powerful – was thundering down the muddy track towards us, on caterpillar treads. Not like the caterpillar treads you get on tanks – these were made from real giant-sized caterpillars. Everything else seemed welded together from hunks of rusty scrap metal. A wonky silver star had been painted on the side.

If I were watching it in a movie I'd say, "Cool design! Nice one!" But this was real life and the ramshackle juggernaut was getting closer, mounting the weird pink grass, heading straight for me, and all I could say was, "Eep!"

"Oh, yeah." Verity was no longer looking so happy. "This is probably another reason why everyone else ran inside."

"What is?"

She glanced sideways at me. "Here comes the Monster Army . . . **to destroy you!**"

"Wha—?" I gulped. "Me? No! This can't be happening . . ."

But it was, of course. With a rusty screech, a hatch in the side of the big, bad vehicle slid open.

RUN FOR IT! RUN! GO ON, RUNNNN!

A huge, powerful-looking figure squeezed out from the army vehicle with some difficulty. He was green, with four red eyes blazing in his face, two holes for a nose and a snarling mouth. Beneath his muddy brown uniform, his arms were bulging with balloon-like muscles. And he had three legs. THREE LEGS.

Clearly he would be able to run way faster than me, and batter me to death, while barely breaking a sweat.

The only thing about him that wasn't truly horrifying was the little peaked cap perched on his head. I reckoned the cap made him look around 4% less scary. But even as I calculated, a gang of green monsters just like him stomped out from inside the tank-thing to join him, and none of them wore caps, so I guessed the cap meant this guy was the leader, which made him about 6% scarier than the rest.

Which basically made him an impressive, if not entirely possible, 102% scary.

"What do we do?" I hissed to Verity.

But my hamster-thing acquaintance was too busy staring, whimpering and shaking her head from side to side to answer. I guess it was her turn to go into a state of shock.

The monster in the cap took a menacing step towards me. "UGH!" he spat. "I am Captain Malevolent P Killgrotty, and YOU are the ugliest thing I ever saw. What are you?"

"I . . . I'm a human, sir," I said weakly.

"I DON'T CARE WHAT YOU ARE!"

Killgrotty shouted.

"But," I said quietly, "you just asked me, so I—"

"Don't interrupt!"

"I wasn't interrupti—"

"**SHADDAP!**" Killgrotty had pulled out a weird-looking pair of goggly binoculars, and stared at me through them. "A **HUMAN**, you say? We can't have a **HUMAN** loose round here. You need to be taken care of. And as for your friend here . . ."

Terrified, I turned to Verity — as if this oversized, overfluffy rodent-monster could possibly help me.

But incredibly, it seemed she could.

Verity had overcome her fear. Now her fur was standing spikily on end, and her eyes were glowing green. "**LEAVE HIM ALOOOOOOOOONE!**" she yelled — and hurled herself at Killgrotty.

"**HUH-?**" Killgrotty hardly had time to react before a hamster-shoe connected with his head. Seriously, it was a heck of a leap – like something out of a (colossally weird) martial arts movie. She landed, then swung round and chopped him behind the knee. Killgrotty fell over with a thump.

His gang of greenies yanked nasty-looking pistols from their pockets. But Verity was all over them, chopping and knocking the guns from their grips, somersaulting back and forth to dodge their grabs and lunges and kicking their legs out from under them. Finally, she cartwheeled back to me in a fluffy blur.

"Whoa!" I spluttered.

"Come on," Verity panted. "**Run!**"

As I sprinted away, I glanced back at Killgrotty – and saw fear, clear on that hideous face. I guessed I'd feel afraid too, if I was as big and tough as him and word got out that I'd been trounced by a hamster!

"I knew there was something nasty going on! Now we know what we're dealing with," Killgrotty told his greenies. "I'll radio HQ for orders. You lot – get after them. We've got to take out the human thing – at all costs!"

I looked at Verity as we raced across the glittering grass. "If they want to take me out of here, I'm happy to let them! Thanks for what you did there, but . . . maybe I should let them catch me? Maybe they could even find what's left of my house?"

"They mean 'take you out' as in—" Verity drew a claw across her throat. "So, run faster!"

I saw the greenies haring after us, three legs carrying each of them in a loping, lop-sided rhythm, and decided Verity's advice was good. I pelted away, sheer terror moving my legs faster than ever before as we reached the mud-track road. There was no cover, nothing to hide

28

behind, no side streets down which we could run. So we just kept running down that road.

"There's only one way for a human to get out of here," said Verity. "We've got to reach my uncle."

"Huh?" I dragged a muddled memory from my overheating mind. "You mean, the humanology-ologist?"

"Yes. We have to find him . . . Urk!" **THUMP!** Verity suddenly tripped and fell flat on her face in the mud, panting wildly for breath. I stopped and rolled her over onto her back. The green glow had faded from her eyes, and her fur had stopped spiking.

"What was I thinking?" she squeaked weakly. "I must've been crazy to start a fight with the Monster Army! Whatever possessed me?"

"Whatever it was, I'm glad it did," I said with feeling. "But, now, Killgrotty's gonna be after you, too."

"S'pose . . . " Verity shrugged. "I couldn't let the first human I ever spotted in REAL LIFE get zapped, could I?"

"Surrender!" bellowed a greenie, leading his mates in the charge for our hides. "You can't run from us!"

"We can, too!" Verity set off again, scurrying away on all fours. I could hardly keep up with her! But we were outrunning the greenies. If we could only keep it up . . .

The muddy track bent sharply to the right. "We're close to the main road," my saviour squeaked. "Maybe we can lose these losers in the traffic, huh, Bob-ob-ob?"

We reached the main road.

To be honest, it wasn't as main as I'd hoped.

"Seriously?" I wheezed. "You couldn't lose anything in this traffic! There isn't any traffic!"

"I just had an idea!" Verity grinned. "That thug said we couldn't run from them, but I bet we could DRIVE from them."

"Brilliant!" I cried. "Do you have a car?"

"No."

"Can you drive?"

"No."

"Not brilliant," I groaned.

"It is, though," she insisted, pointing to a rusty blue contraption rattling along the road towards us. "We càn catch a bus!"

Verity scurried out into the road – directly into the blue vehicle's path! "Hey! Request stop!" She waved her paws, wiggled from side to side and jumped up and down. The big blue bus showed no sign of slowing down – or trying to steer around her. My only ally was about to be squished ...!

"Look out!" I staggered after Verity, arms flapping above my head, ready to whisk her to safety. But then, with a hissing screech of ancient-sounding brakes, the bus finally skidded to a stop.

"Nice work, partner!" Verity beamed at me and ran up to the passenger door, knocking on the glass. "Excuse me!" she called. "This human being called Bob-ob-ob and I need to get on your bus to escape a bunch of very angry soldiers who are right behind us . . ."

"**AUUUGHHHH!**" The bus windows exploded as panic-stricken passengers hurled themselves from their seats and out into the muddy road. Then the doors opened — and a tall, thin, yellow monster in a stained grey driver's uniform burst from inside, screaming.

"Have the bus!" he hollered. "Please, just take it! Take it!" With that, he joined the charge of petrified passengers across the road and onto the track, heading back the way we'd come. The gang of three-legged greenies appeared from around the bend and promptly collided with the panic-stricken crowd, falling down in a dusty tangle.

My legs felt wobbly and weak as I stared after them. "They really are scared of humans, aren't they?"

Verity nodded cheerfully as she climbed on board the bus. "They probably thought you were going to fire toxic waste out of your nose. Everyone knows humans can totally fire toxic waste from their noses."

"Huh?" I joined her on the yuck-smelling bus. "We can't, though!"

"Aww, c'mon, Bob-ob-ob." She got into the driver's seat and started studying the switches and dials around the steering wheel. "My uncle took a video through his humanoscope of this human man who made a noise like a squeelsquog and shot radioactive sludge out through his nose. It went viral on GooTube . . . "

"What? You mean he sneezed?"

"Bob-ob-ob, what is this human thing called 'sneezed'?"

"Forget it! Please, concentrate on working this thing!" I watched, helpless and horrified as the greenies on the track tossed hapless bus-passengers aside like rag dolls and got back to their big, ugly feet. Suddenly, the bus lurched backwards with a splutter of smoke and almost threw me out through a shattered window. "Whoaaa! Careful!"

"Sorry." Verity pulled a lever beside the steering wheel, grinned, and rubbed her paws together. "Ah. Of course! That's it!"

"You've learned how to drive this thing?"

"No, but I think this switch works the ticket machine."

"Arrrrrgh!" I clutched my head with both hands. "Killgrotty's thugs will be here any second!"

Verity squeaked. "Quick, Bob-ob-ob, hold them off with toxic waste nose power."

"I told you, HUMANS CAN'T . . . Wait a sec." I poked my head through one of the shattered windows. Through the kicked-up dust, I saw the greenies were almost on top of us. "Stay back!" I yelled. "Or I . . . I'll totally spray you with my toxic-waste nose!"

At once, the greenies came to a scuffling stop, swapping uncertain looks.

"Yeah, now you're thinking!" I tried to wave my nose at them in a threatening manner (which wasn't easy), wondering if I should fake a sneeze – although I guessed the greenies would be unimpressed by my lack of, er, greenies. "I'm warning you – I'm fully loaded and ready to blow . . . OHHHHH!"

With a screech of spinning wheels, the bus pulled away, throwing up dirt into the greenies' faces. "**Yeee-haahhh!**" Verity cried. "Eat our dust!"

I fell back into a seat, cringing as I discovered that it was still sticky from whoever/whatever had sat in it last. "You did it, Verity! Can we go and find your uncle now, and see if he knows where my house ended up?"

"Abso-nibblin'-lootly," Verity agreed as the bus zoomed down the main road. "Unless we, you know, crash on the way, cos I don't know how to steer, or brake, or understand traffic lights, or stuff." She paused. "I remember how to give you a ticket, though. I think."

My heart was sinking faster than the Creature from the Black Lagoon after a heavy lunch. "How far is it to your uncle's?"

"Hmm, let me think . . ." To my horror, Verity closed her eyes and stroked her chin – just as we drove through a crossroads! A monster car swerved desperately to avoid us and smashed into a cart thing at the side of the road, which blew up. I watched through the side window as the driver was thrown skyhigh with his bottom on fire, smashing through the window of a nearby house – which immediately collapsed, thundering to the ground in a storm of yellow bricks. The bricks blew up, engulfed in flames, and four monsters hopped out of the flattened house, clutching their smoking body-parts.

I watched the carnage, speechless, as Verity finally opened her eyes again and smiled at me. "I think Uncle's place is only about eighty blonks away! As long as we don't get lost. Hey, where are we, anyway? Whoops, don't forget your ticket!" She pulled the lever and a slip of stained paper ground out of a slot in the dashboard. "Fear not, Bob-ob-ob, it's free. On the house! Or on the bus, anyway . . ."

"I wish I wasn't on the bus," I muttered, sitting back down, one hand clutching my stomach, the other holding onto my seat. I looked out of the back window. How long before Killgrotty's armoured car vroomed after us?

Or some other horror, that we didn't even know about yet?

Or that monster we'd just blown through a window with his bum on fire?

All I had on my side was an oversized hamster with no road sense.

I had a feeling this was going to be a long eighty blonks.

CHAPTER 5

DOWN, DOWN, DOWN

I learned a few things in that bus:

1) Monster traffic lights have thirteen colours, twelve of which are different shades of red.

2) Verity doesn't know what any of these signals indicate, except, "One of the red ones means slow down."

3) Luckily, traffic cops are few and far between around here, or we would've been totally busted ages ago. We smashed into six cars, two trucks, three lamp posts, and something that looked like a giant pink horse with the head of a doughnut and went "**0000000000000000000**" when we ran over its tail.

4) Monster neighbourhoods up on the top level are kind of like human neighbourhoods — houses, shops, offices, schools, parks, libraries; all that stuff, only monster-style. The parks are artificial, to stop certain monsters eating them.

5) Verity feels very lucky to live up here because it's quite posh. The nine lower levels of Monsterland – or, Deep Monster Territories, as they are known – get nastier, smellier, and way more dangerous the deeper down you go.

6) Verity's uncle lives three levels beneath this one (about 40% scarier – great!).

I had visions of Monsterland as some kind of giant department store. "So how do we get down to your uncle's?" I asked. "Is there, like, a big lift or something?"

"Lift?" Verity frowned. "What is this human thing called 'lift', Bob-ob-ob?"

"You know, like, an elevator. A big machine that carries

you up and down."

"Oh. I see. '*Lift*'. Brilliant." She looked round at me, baring her beavery teeth in a big grin. "Yes, we have something like a 'lift', Bob-ob-ob. We have *nogglodons* – big platforms on chains that go up and down, pulled by enormous red-spotted monsters known as *nogglodon operators* . . ."

I pointed to the (now cracked) windscreen. "Please look at the road. Remember what happened last time—?"

WHUMP! A wrinkly grey monster was suddenly spread-eagled over the windscreen, looking confused.

"Oh, yeah! **THAT** happened." Verity hit the windscreen wipers, and the grey monster yelped as he was swept off and into a conveniently placed pile of trash cans at the side of the road. I saw him shake his fist at us as we drove out of sight.

"Poor old monster," I murmured.

"Don't worry, he's okay. He's not old, he's just wrinkly. And wrinkly monsters are tough."

"How old are you?" I asked.

Verity considered. "I'm pretty young, I think. Kind of like you."

I sighed. "So are we heading for one of these nogglodon things?"

"Nogg*lo*don," said Verity, correcting the way I said it.

"Sorry. Are we heading for one of these nogg*lo*don things?"

"**Nogg**lodon."

"You just said it was 'nogg*lo*don'."

"No, Bob-ob-ob, I said it was nogglo**don**."

"What?"

"Nogglo**don**."

"Then why did you say it was '**nogg**lodon' before?"

"I didn't, Bob-ob-ob."

I gritted my teeth. "My name is Bob."

"Bob-ob-ob."

"Bob."

"Bob-ob-ob-nnnn."

"Bob-ob-ob-nnnn? Where did the 'n's come from?!"

"You humans," chuckled Verity. Swerving sharply right without braking, she smashed through a fence onto a narrow road. "I can't help it if you say some of your words funny. Like 'Bob-ob-ob' and 'nogg**lo**don'."

"All right. Sorry." I took a deep breath and sighed it out again. "Are we heading for one of these nogg**lo**dons?"

"**Nogg**lodons."

"HOWEVER YOU SAY IT!" I cried. "ARE WE HEADING FOR ONE?"

"No."

"ARRRRRRRRRGH!"

The bus cracked through a cobwebbed old barrier, and the road got narrower still. It got bumpier, too — the whole bus started to shake like a puppy having a bad dream. Verity pulled on a seatbelt. Why now? I wondered. Then a mega-pothole made me bang my head on the back of the seat. For a moment, I thought that was why everything had gone dark. But no, the lights came back on, then went out, then came back on again.

Daylight was flashing on and off.

"It's almost night-time," Verity reported. "Since there is no sun down here, only skybulbs, the skybulbs start flashing for a few minutes each night to warn monsters everywhere that it's nearly end-of-day. Time to sleep . . . hang up the hongles . . . watch the late-night perigosto races . . ."

"And crash into even more innocent monsters unless you find the headlamps on this thing." I hugged myself; this crazy world was scary enough by 'daylight'. The idea of thundering along this rutted road in pitch blackness . . .

"Look, Verity," I tried again, "if we're not making for one of those platform lifts, then *why* aren't we?"

"Because it's too obvious!" Verity tapped her snout knowingly. "Killgrotty is bound to have army trucks and soldiers and tanks and bazookoos and stuff at every nogglodon on this level. But I'll bet he hasn't thought to guard the disused *back* way down to Level Four."

"Why wouldn't he?" I wondered.

She tapped her nose again and winked. "Because it's so crazily dangerous, no one in their right minds would ever take it."

I swallowed hard. "And that's the way we're taking?"

"Yes." Verity pressed on the brakes to slow our jerky journey. "It's basically a big hole at the side of this old, disused road, hidden by mashberry leaves. You'd better hang on tight. And if we time things right, no one will be able to see us go."

"Huh?" I hugged my seat for dear life as the lights clunked off, and all was dark.

"There we are!" said Verity, her eyes glowing green in the blackness. "Or rather . . . HERE we are! Hole ahead. Going down!"

The road was gone as quickly as the light. Suddenly we were freefalling. Into oblivion . . .

CHAPTER 6

SO! THIS IS OBLIVION, HUH? IT'S RUBBISH!

"**Wheeeeeeeeeeeeeeeeeeeeeeee!**" sang Verity, as our bus plummeted through darkness.

"Nooo-ooooo-oooooo-ooooooo!" I joined in.

My heart had flown up my throat, and I was glad of the sticky seat now — it held me in place and stopped me smacking into the roof. I had an awful flashback of falling through the window of my tumbling home.

WHOOSH! A band of glowing green whizzed past the windows. **WHOOOOSH!** A blur of purple. Were these monster levels we were passing on our way down? If so, after one more **WHOOOSH!** and a smear of colour (ooh, orange now) we would—

WHUMMMMMPH!

It was a soft landing, like crashing into a giant marshmallow. Except it wasn't a marshmallow – it looked like a mushroom. First we sank deep into it. Then the marshmallow-shroom boinged us back up like a sticky trampoline. *Up-down-up-down* we went, over and over, like a bouncy ball slowly coming to rest.

"Whew!" Verity said, upside down in a tangle in her seatbelt. "We made it!"

"Verity," I said weakly, sliding from my seat. "Next time we travel between levels, can we please take the nogglo*don*?"

"You mean, nog*glo*don."

"Shut up."

Rubbing my eyes, I realised there was a burnt-orange glow outside the windows. The skybulbs were switched on down here, but they were much dimmer. I scrambled up and looked out through the windscreen into the thick gloom.

"Welcome to the northern zone of Deep Monster Territory Level Four," said Verity. "Landing here brings us out just around the corner from Uncle Voshto."

I smiled despite myself. "With the way you drive, I'm impressed you managed to find it first time."

"I've been coming here since I was a little nibbler, Bob-ob-ob." Verity pressed a button and the bus doors fell off, clattering to the ground. "Well. Let's go!"

So we did.

It was dank and chilly down here. As my eyes got used to the gloom, I saw a barren, sinister wasteland covered in spongy, sticky mushrooms, some low-level, some vast like the giant one we crashed into. It stretched on for miles! The air smelled like burnt rubber. Tatty tinsel creepers wound around concrete pillars that reached up into the shadowy space far above. Toadstool bonfires had been lit

here and there, but they did little to light the place, and even less to warm it, and left smoke hanging in the air like mist. The whole place seemed mouldy, smelly and falling apart.

"So this is where the monsters not as nice as the ones up on the top level live," I shivered. "Why does your uncle stay here?"

"He's hiding out where no one would think of looking for him, while he works on a top-secret project," Verity explained. "Not many monsters come here for fun. Hey, look! That's where Uncle Voshto's staying – a tavern called The Severed Arm."

She pointed a paw at a distant building that stood

apart from the half-shadow of the houses beyond. It looked part-spooky-old-castle and part-nightclub, zinging with neon lights. I felt homesick for normal sights – then imagined how sick I'd feel if I had to live somewhere like this instead! Oh, my poor house! Could it really be scattered all over everywhere?

Verity led me towards the jagged silhouette of The Severed Arm by a roundabout route, dashing between giant mushrooms for cover. The ground sucked at my trainers. The bonfire flames danced like living things. Every now and then a growl or a groan floated through the air, and Verity would hold very still. I decided to do the same thing. I had the feeling that I was being watched on all sides by unknown things.

"We'd better move quickly," Verity murmured. "I don't much like it down here."

"Where did all you monsters come from?" I murmured as we sheltered under an especially enormous and unpleasant-smelling toadstool. "I mean, so many different kinds . . . "

"We've been on the planet as long as humans have. You must have heard the Really Old stories from the lands of

Ancient Eejit and Greasy?"

"Egypt and Greece, you mean?"

"What are these human things, Egypt and—?"

"Never mind," I said quickly. "You're basically saying that the old monsters like the Sphinx and the Minotaur and the Cyclops . . . they were all real?"

"Abso-chompin'-lootly they were," Verity said. "In the Really Old Days there were lots of monsters up top, living alongside your ancestors. Well, dying alongside them, usually. You humans! I mean, what about Odysseus – he was like a serial monster-killer!" She tutted. "Well, anyway, some time in the fifth century, all the monsters moved down here to Terra Monstra, out of sight."

I felt suddenly spooked, and glanced back at the old bus. It seemed a long way behind us already, a wreck washed up in the grotty sea of fungus. "But what caused them to suddenly hide?"

Verity looked at me, dark-eyed. "My uncle can explain it better than me. He's a professor and stuff."

"And he can get me out before Killgrotty has me *taken* out?" I added, seeking reassurance.

"I'm sure he can, Bob-ob-ob. Though it might be quite a

trek." Verity paused beside a huge grey toadstool to wash her whiskers. "There used to be loads of easy ways in and out of the hidden monster-lands to the human world above. But they've all been paved over now." She sighed, and set off again. "Some monsters were stuck outside, unable to return home. Like Bigfoot – he gets so bored wandering the Rocky mountains, he has to jump out and flash his bum saying '**Oo! Oo!**' at startled tourists for a laugh."

"What about the Loch Ness Monster?" I asked.

"She never shows her bum, Bob-ob-ob! She has her dignity."

Verity's revelations were fantastic, but with all the weirdness I was already experiencing, I found myself accepting them quite easily. Perhaps the stinky smoke fumes were turning my brain to mush – they were getting stronger the closer we got to the tavern. I stopped walking (what the flip was I walking into?) and with a nervous glance at Verity, surveyed the ruined pub before me. Its ragged turrets stretched very nearly to the dirt 'sky' overhead. Smoke wafted past its neon lights.

One sign flashed in different shades of green:

THE SEVERED ARM
TOP NITESPOT

There were other signs flashing in the murk, mostly in blood-red and crimson:

TOUGH MONSTERS ONLY

read one.

IF YOU BLEED ON OUR FLOOR, CLEAN IT UP YOURSELF
OR DIE!

another instructed.

Suddenly, Verity's ears pricked and she turned round in a panic, shooing me behind a giant 'shroom. I heard the squeal of a heavy door and sounds of struggle.

"What's going on?" I hissed, eyes watering in a gust of smoke. "I can't see!"

Verity's eyes were keener than mine. "Well, Bob-ob-ob, a

big, purple monster with three arms just came out from the tavern."

I gulped as I heard a succession of splashes. "What's he doing?"

"Beating up six bigger monsters and throwing them into a stagnant pond."

Drying my eyes, I peered out from behind the mushroom and winced. "He must be The Severed Arm's bouncer."

"What is this human thing called 'bouncer'?"

"You know, he stands at the door of a club and sort of keeps control. Says who can come in and who has to get out."

"I never saw one here before," said Verity. "Normally I just sneak inside and scurry upstairs — the monsters are all too busy fighting to take any notice."

I nodded nervously. "Well, I'm sure this bouncer only beat up those monsters because they did something bad."

"RIGHT!" The bouncer screamed with rage at the giant thugs in the septic pool, waving three enormous fists. "The next time you ask me what time it is, I'll tear you apart WITHOUT MERCY!" Then he smoothed out his leather trousers and stomped back to stand guard over

The Severed Arm's heavy wooden door. "When is someone gonna give me a PROPER fight?"

I cowered under the mushroom cap. "Er . . . is there a back door?"

Verity shook her head. "Afraid not."

"Perfect," I muttered. "So, if we want to reach your uncle, we've got to get through that ultra-violent maniac first!"

CHAPTER 7

ATTACK OF THE UNKNOWN FEARSOME MONSTER OF FEAR

Verity and I stared at the huge, burly monster blocking our only way into the tavern.

"It doesn't look like this thing is going to listen to reason." I gave her an encouraging smile. "I know violence isn't the answer . . . but you trounced Killgrotty and his whole gang of greenies."

"I still don't know how I did that." Verity shrugged. "Anyway, all I really did was buy us time to run away. This time we want to stay. And that Bouncer will just follow us in and crush us." She considered. "Maybe you could scare him away with the toxic nose thing?"

"HUMANS DON'T DO THAT—" I burst out impatiently, to frantic shushing. "Sorry. I've just had a gutful of being the only human round here . . ." An idea crawled cautiously into my head. "Hey! Speaking of guts, do you think these monsters eat the mushrooms?"

"Sure." Verity nibbled a bit of our cover. "Yum! Why?"

I looked at her. "Maybe we could make a special delivery?"

Minutes later, our plan was prepared.

WHAT COULD I POSSIBLY MEAN, EH, READER? I SHALL REVEAL ALL . . . SOON. VERY SOON. IN FACT – NOW.

Preparation basically involved Verity using her beaver teeth to gnaw a neat line up the side of the massive mushroom, allowing me to crawl inside. I held the spongy edges together as discreetly as possible, and (with much difficulty and squeaking), Verity hefted me up in her arms.

"**Oi!**" I heard the big purple bouncer snarl. "You with the mushroom?"

"Hey, monster, how you nibbling?" I heard Verity say. "Coooooool! Yeah. Punched any good faces, lately?"

"**NO**," he snarled. "Only bad faces like yours."

"Ha!" Verity squeaked nervously. "Well . . . this is a special delivery. For the kitchen monsters. They are expecting this marvellous mushroom. In one piece."

"Why?" the bouncer demanded. "Is it poisonous?"

"Er, no."

"**WHY NOT?**" he bawled. "What kind of a lousy mushroom delivery monster **ARE YOU?**"

Through a crack in the mushroom I saw him pull all three fists back, ready to serve a triple helping of knuckle sandwich.

"No!" I burst out through the spongy mushroom and fell in a heap on the floor. "Ta-daaa," I said weakly.

The bouncer blinked. "Thought you said it wasn't poisoned?"

The plan had failed — it was time to think up a new one. Fast. "I'm your, er, singing human-o-gram!"

"My what?"

I nodded. "I turn up dressed as a human and, er . . . sing a song to you."

The bouncer had screwed up his face in disgust, as if his ears could taste words and mine tasted like dog poo. "Sing? **SING?**"

"Yes!" said Verity quickly, "because, um, I work for B.U.M. Magazine."

The bouncer raised his fists again. **"BUM?"**

"Yes, you know, B.U.M., short for Big Ugly Monster. And I've brought this mushroom and singing human-o-gram to, er, celebrate the fact that you have been voted, um, Big Ugly Monster of the Year by our readers."

"I have?" The Bouncer lowered his fists a fraction. "Who nominated me?"

"Umm . . . Your mum." Verity nodded. "And your gran."

"What, even after I tried to blow them up that time?" The bouncer's eyes welled up with happy tears. "I . . . I never knew they cared! Oi! Mum! Gran!"

I swapped a panicked look with Verity. "Er, no need to bother them…"

"Shaddap! I'm gonna tell my mates, an' all." The bouncer leaned through the doorway to reveal a dark, smoky space. It reeked of sweat, cabbage and overpowering wind. "Ere, everyone! You'll never guess what – I'm **BUM** of the Year!"

"You wot?" came a grunt from inside.

"**BUM!**" the bouncer yelled.

"Who you calling a bum, son?" someone shouted. "You wanna fight?"

"**COME ON THEN!**" the bouncer screamed, and charged inside.

In less than a second, the sound of smashing glass, heavy blows and breaking furniture erupted from The Severed Arm like an explosion – quickly followed by a real explosion as a small bomb detonated. A wave of heat singed Verity's fur and the shockwaves knocked us to the ground.

"Now's our chance!" she squeaked, as a yellow, lumpy monster was knocked cartwheeling out of the tavern.

"Let's sneak inside and creep upstairs!"

"Through that lot?" I stared despairingly. "They'll slaughter us!"

But Verity was already scurrying inside. I took a deep breath and followed her into the smoky, stinky, candlelit den. Jostling monsters kicked and clobbered each other to a soundtrack of grunts and '**OOF!**'s. Barstools flew over my head. A huge bottle smashed just beside me – its contents making the carpet smoke before a weird, doglike monster lapped it all up, belched out flames, and set fire to the legs of a tall monster beside him. I rolled to get clear – straight into a swipe from the thick tail of an even thicker-looking monster. It knocked me backwards into a green, slimy octopus thing, who lifted me into the air and tossed me against the wall.

"Verity?" I cried, but couldn't see her amid the heaving scrum of maniac monsters.

"**Hewwwww-man, is it?**" croaked a scorched and sooty female monster with four wide eyes and incredibly big fists. "**What're you doing here, hewwwww-man? You want a piece of us? Huh?**"

"Noooo, I am a singing human-o-graaaaaaaam," I tried

to sing, but my voice was so wobbly and faint I could hardly hear myself. "Do not kill meeeeee," I crooned desperately, "do not kill me, dooooooo nooooooooot kiiiiiiiilllllll . . . meeeeee . . ."

The beasts closed in around me. A dragon-thing with a machine gun. A cow-monster covered in spikes with a blue udder on her head. A huge lobster-like life-form with a hand grenade in each claw (or a claw-grenade in each hand?) ready to pull the pin with its sabre-sharp teeth . . .

"That's enough, boys and girls!" came a cry from the smoky darkness beyond them. "LOOK AT ME!"

The high-pitched command rang out at ear-whumping volume. The brawling monsters turned to see who was calling.

And as they did so, they froze.

I don't mean they just stood still. I mean, they literally turned into blue and frosty statues where they stood (or crouched over their unconscious victims, or lay sprawled on the floor). I started to turn to see what on Earth could have done this.

"No," came the girl's voice again. "Don't look yet. We need to get ready . . . "

"Er, what?" Dread's cold fingers pinched at my spine. Where had Verity got to? Had she been ice-blasted too?

"There, now," said the girl. I heard footsteps coming towards me. "You can look . . . LOOK OVER HERE..."

My eyes were tightly shut. Whatever it was, I wasn't looking. I was NOT looking!

"LOOK!" the girl wailed, drawing closer. And closer . . .

CHAPTER 8

SNAKES ALIVE!

"Oh, come on, DO look over here," came the voice. Now its mysterious owner was closer, I found she sounded less scary. In fact, she sounded quite plummy and posh. "The girls and I are looking particularly stylish today!"

I risked opening my eyes.

And stared.

The person before me was wearing enormous dark glasses with round lenses, and a paint-splodged apron over a white blouse with puffy sleeves. She looked human enough, besides her green-tinged skin and the hooked claws on her fingers and thumbs. Oh, and the forked tail snaking out of the back of her black leggings. Oh (again), and the wild array of snakes growing out of her head.

Yes. Snakes, swaying and coiling, some with a little beret on their head, some with a mini pair of shades, some with a silk scarf tied delicately beneath their jaw.

"What the flip?!" I breathed.

"Hiyaaaaaa!" She waggled her fingers at me in a coy

wave. "You're new around here, aren't you?"

My mouth was too busy flapping open and shut to form much of a reply, as the memory of a Year Six English lesson pinged into my mind. "You're . . . a gorgon!"

The green girl grinned and her snakes stood up, hissing happily and nodding to each other. "Yes, I am! My name is Zola. Perhaps you've heard of me?"

"Gorgon . . . zola?" I frowned. Wasn't that a cheese?

Funnily enough, my mind didn't linger on the 'Zola' part of all this. It lingered on the word 'GORGON' and the old Greek legends of the evil gorgon Medusa and her sisters who could turn people to stone with a

YES, IT'S TRUE. I AM LEGENDARY!

single look . . .

"What do you think of my still life, hmm?" Zola leaned towards me, enquiringly.

"Your . . . what?"

"All this!" She gestured round at the frozen scene.

"Um . . . aren't still lifes normally fruit and flowers and stuff . . . ?"

"In the name of Athena . . . !" Zola started fanning herself. "Goddess above, you know about art! You're artistic, aren't you? You've just got to be."

I frowned. "Excuse me?"

By now the gorgon was jumping up and down with excitement. "Okay, okay. Here's the test: What's paint?"

"Huh?"

"Tell me what paint is!"

"It's coloured stuff you . . . paint with?"

"HE KNOWS ABOUT PAINT! No one down here has any concept of the stuff, but THIS FUNNY-LOOKING THING does!" The gorgon grabbed me and danced about, her snakes wiggling and trying to kiss me. "HE KNOWS PAINNNNNNT! He's an artist!"

"Get off!" I cried, wrenching free. I tried to back away towards a dingy staircase – then tripped over something warm and fluffy and fell to the filthy floor.

"Bob-ob-ob?" I heard a familiar squeaking groan in my ear.

"Verity! Thank flip I've found you!"

Her black eyes flickered open and she gazed at me. "What is this human thing called 'Flip'?"

"Never mind that. We've got company."

"I know." She jabbed a claw to a squid-like thing beside her, which had frozen with its tentacles raised and its face to the bar. "I was trying to find you when that thing got me with a sucker-punch."

"You mean it hit you when you weren't looking?" asked Zola.

"No, it punched me with its suckers. Hey, who said that ...?" Verity suddenly noticed Zola and clutched onto my arm. "What's going on here?"

"For a start, you're cutting off my circulation," I gasped through gritted teeth.

"She's a gorgon!" Verity twittered. "Look! She's turned everyone into stone!"

"Excuse me! I think you'll find I've got a little more imagination than that!" huffed Zola. "I actually turned them into an ice, slush and frost-glitter statement piece." She smiled soppily at me. "Right, arty boy?"

"Drop the act, sweetheart," Verity scowled. "I know you gorgons. The only art you go for is statues. You turn other monsters into stone – forever! How come you're not with the rest of them down on Level Six?"

"I'm . . . not like the other gorgons . . ." Zola looked suddenly crestfallen. "The problem is, I can't turn anyone into stone. The Council of Gorgons chucked me out of our land for being too soft and sensitive." She gave a theatrical sigh and did some strange, ungainly ballet steps before leaning against the bar. "That's why I'm stuck here, so far from home."

Verity sniffed. "I suppose not being able to turn people to stone is a bit of a disadvantage for a gorgon."

"So to make up for it, you're . . ." I looked round doubtfully at the frozen bodies. "Artistic."

"You noticed! Well, you are a fellow artist, of course." She beamed, and her snakes intertwined. "I never quite know WHAT'S going to happen when I let loose my gorgon glare. I turned a monster into cardboard, once. And another into a big bowl of green porridge. But this time I think I've excelled myself! Don't you just LOVE what I've done?"

"Er . . ." I looked at my feet awkwardly. "Have you killed them?"

"Oh, noooooooooooooooo!" Her snakes gave a scandalised gasp. "No, no, no, no, no, no, no, no. Anything I transform turns back to normal in about five minutes." She sighed again. "That's another reason why I was thrown out of Level Six. No good at killing things, see?"

Verity was still watching Zola with disapproval. "So how did you end up here?"

"The landlord hired me to break up the worst fights before the whole place collapses." Zola shook her head, and her snakes did the same. "It's not the happiest life. In fact, it stinks. But I dream of earning enough money to put on a big gallery show somewhere, and being discovered as a famous artist!"

Verity looked dubious. "Even if you had the cash, it'd take a miracle for the monsters round here to become art lovers."

"How much do you need?" I wondered.

Zola started counting on her clawed fingers. "About three hundred plogoos."

"How many plogoos do you have?"

"One." Zola shrugged. "Still, the old fella upstairs pays me a zonk or two extra to freeze everyone now and then so he can do his experiments in peace . . ."

"That's right," came a wavery old voice from the top of the stairs, "I do!"

The voice made me jump. I saw yet another weird monster. He looked like a benign blue eel, wrinkly and well worn, with three-lensed specs for his three eyes, rearing up on a whole load of legs, leaning on a well-gnawed cane.

"Uncle!" Verity scampered up the stairs and licked his face. "Uncle Voshto, it's so good to see you."

"Verity? Is that Verity?" The old monster peered at her. "Goodness, child, it's about time! I've been waiting so long for you to visit!"

"Sorry, Uncle. Sometimes it's hard to get away. But look what I've brought with me!"

She pointed to me so proudly I couldn't really object to her calling me a 'what' rather than a 'who'.

"A human? Here! A HUMAN?" He took a step towards me, muttering under his breath, his legs trembling like skinny blue blancmanges "Well, well, it's just as I anticipated. A human has got through!"

"A human?" Zola's snakes stood on end as she cowered back. "You're not going to fire toxic waste out of your—?"

"No," I cut in.

"You mean nose," Verity corrected me.

"You can't stay here, boy!" Voshto was getting agitated. "Dear me, no. You'll be starting wars—"

"I won't!" I said.

"Polluting the place—"

"I won't!" I cried.

"Eating all the wimblebeasts."

"What?"

"Infecting innocent monsters with hideous human diseases . . ."

I paused. "Er, I'll try not to."

"Hmm. I think I know what to do with you. Come, the pair of you – to my secret workshop!"

"Yes, you'd better go quickly," Zola said sadly. "These

brawlers will be thawing out and springing back to life at any moment." She pulled out a camera and started taking pictures of the scene. "Just a few pics for the scrapbook. Don't want to forget this little installation . . ."

I, on the other hand, wanted to forget it as quickly as possible – and so I was very happy to run up the stairs to join Voshto. "Um, see you later, Zola," I called back as I went. "Thanks for saving us!"

Zola half smiled and put her hands on her hips. "I'd prefer it if you thanked me for making an incredible artistic statement. See you soon, artsy human boy!"

"Bit of a bighead, isn't she?" Verity grumbled as she bustled her uncle back up the steps and along the creaky wooden landing. I jumped at a sudden hubbub of voices as the pub's patrons did indeed spring back to life. But at least their racket covered the noise of Uncle Voshto ushering us into his workshop, shutting the door and accidentally banging into a coffee table full of bottles and beakers, which fell everywhere.

"Well, well. A real human!" Voshto prodded me with his cane. "What a shame we can't keep him for proper study. But I know how he got here. I've been listening to the news reports on the radio-box. What a scene he must've caused! And now you're involved too, Verity, eh?"

"We're in trouble deep, Unc," Verity agreed. "Captain Killgrotty himself is after us both."

"Oh!" Voshto let out a fearful groan. "You must get this human away from Terra Monstra as quickly as possible — then perhaps Killgrotty will forgive you."

"I'm up for that," I said with feeling, gazing round Voshto's workshop. It was part grimy hovel, part Frankenstein's laboratory. Wooden tables heaved beneath the weight of scientific clutter. Cupboards spilled secret experiments onto a floor carpeted with sheets of crumpled notepaper, which were marked with mindboggling equations. Beside a broken bed and a very dirty toilet I saw a huge, squat red tube, pointing up at the mouldy ceiling. It was connected to an oversized TV screen that showed a very familiar street . . . and a gaping hole in the ground where once there had been a house.

My house.

"What a hole!" I gasped.

Voshto looked cross. "Yes, well, I haven't hoovered, lately."

"He's talking about what you're looking at through the humanoscope," Verity explained.

"Ah, yes. Yes, I feared a human or two might end up here as a result of that, er, upheaval."

I frowned. "What upheaval?"

"My special scanners picked it up! A huge energy surge from the monster world into yours — and back again! But first things first, human boy." Voshto peered at me. "Your house."

"My *poor* house! It must be scattered all over this crazy world of yours."

"More likely it's been drawn right to the very bottom." Old Voshto nodded thoughtfully. "You were lucky, you know. Since the back ways between our two worlds have long since been blocked, there's only one way a human could travel to Terra Monstra safely — and that's within an outer plasmic shell of brickwork, wood and glass that's been exposed to eerinium."

"My house is made of brickwork, wood and glass . . ." I scratched my head. "But what's eerinium?"

"The eerie energy that powers our underground world!" Voshto said impatiently. "I believe your house was built on a tiny fault-line between the human world and ours. If enough eerinium leaked out through the crack into the foundations of your home ..." He shook his head, touched his cane to his lips. "After many years, so much eerinium leaking into the area would eventually cause a *weirdwind* – a trans-dimensional tornado strong enough to blow the house straight through the magical barriers that shield Terra Monstra from human detection."

I struggled to take everything in. "So ... it's just my bad luck I happened to live in this house right on top of the weirdy leak thing? And you think it's been pulled down into Monsterland?"

"Right down to the lowest levels, where the ancient eerinium lies thickest. It's lucky you fell out when you did, and luckier still that someone as kind and human-fond as Verity found you."

"*Lickier* still, too!" Verity slurped my cheek fondly, ignoring my grimace. "So, Unc – how are we going to get the human home, huh?"

"Well, I believe there IS a way, but ..." Voshto regarded me thoughtfully. "Do you trust him, Verity? Are you certain he is what he seems to be?"

Verity nodded. "Abso-nibblin'-totally."

"Only, all manner of strange and sinister forces would love to get hold of my research!" Voshto seemed gripped by a sudden passion (or possibly wind). "For so long now, I have been peeping into forbidden corners of understanding! Gathering secret knowledge! Piecing together the evidence from ancient relics and half-translated scrolls – *finally* making an indescribably important discovery . . ." The weird professor stooped and rummaged on the floor (for quite some time) until finally he snatched up a sheet with a scribbled drawing on it. "Yes, WHAT a discovery. After a lifetime's effort, I have learned the location of . . . THIS."

I studied the picture. "Er . . . a worm wearing a bikini?"

"What? Oh. Sorry. Where did that come from?" Voshto blushed and turned the paper round. "I mean . . . THIS."

Now I was looking at a drawing of a many-sided gemstone, sitting on a cushion.

"What is it, Unc?" Verity whispered. "Tell us."

"THIS . . . is the Humamon Star Jewel." Voshto spoke softly, reverently. "It belonged to the greatest human magician that ever lived. One thousand five hundred years ago, he used the jewel's uncanny powers to help create Terra Monstra beneath the earth . . ."

I found myself caught up in the spookiness of the moment. "What magician?"

"We monsters call him the Great Divider or the Lord of the Lair." Voshto smiled and nodded. "But you, child . . . you would call him *Merlin*."

CHAPTER 9

AND THE ARTISTIC GORGON MAKES THREE

"Merlin?" I spluttered. "Seriously? I thought he was, like, made up."

Voshto frowned. "I don't believe he wore make-up. But surely his private life is his own affair."

"No, I mean, I thought he wasn't real. That he was just a story."

"Many real things from those long ago days are believed now to be nothing more than stories." Voshto shook his eelish head. "But as sure as

A STORY?! ME?! I DO TURN UP IN STORIES, SUCH AS THAT SPLENDID EFFORT *MAGIC INK*... HEY, WHAT DO YOU MEAN THIS ISN'T THE PLACE TO PLUG MY BOOKS?

78

bishtops are anthroblobs, Merlin created the Humamon Star Jewel as a gift for his master, King Arthur. And what a gift! According to ancient wisdom:

> "Whoe'er doth hold
> the Star Jewel in their hand
> Whate'er their heart's desire
> may truly be
> Good or bad, receive it
> so they shall
> In less time than it takes
> a Nog to wee."

"Oooooooh," cooed Verity.

I looked blank.

"A nog is, like, totally famous for doing really fast wees," she clarified.

"Right," I said dubiously. "So, Merlin made this jewel for Arthur. Then what?"

"Well, there were many monsters on the Earth in those times," Voshto revealed. "And almost immediately, the jewel was stolen by the worst of all — an evil monster named Bosstradamus."

"Who?" I said.

"Bosstradamus had a run-in or two with Arthur, and her heart's desire was to banish that mighty human king to a hellish underground pit, where he would be trapped forever more."

"Ouch," I said, sympathetically.

"But that evil she-monster did not know that Merlin had charmed the jewel so it could never hurt Arthur. Her dark wish backfired, and the jewel transported *her* to that hellish pit deep underground instead."

Verity seemed entranced by the tale, nibbling her claws. "Couldn't she wish herself out again?"

"It was useless to her from the moment she wished harm on Arthur," said Voshto. "In anger, she threw it away . . . And the mighty king was so angry to lose his magic jewel that in his temper he desired to rid the world of monsters forever."

"So Merlin created Terra Monstra and banished all the monsters down here," said Verity.

Her uncle nodded. "He used the powers of the jewel, combined with eerinium in the earth. What a wizard he truly was."

"But why would Merlin leave the jewel here?" I wondered. "Why not take it back with him?"

"I don't have ALL the answers." Voshto seemed uppity all of a sudden. "My theory is that the Bosstradamus business made Merlin realise the jewel was too powerful to fall into the wrong hands. After all, if evil monsters could steal it, so too could evil humans – and that could prove far worse. So he hid it in a place of safety knowing that one day he could reclaim it . . ." Voshto moved to a drawer stuffed full of papers and pulled out a notepad. "However, I have set out to reclaim it first! I have worked out the jewel's location and the best way to reach it. It's all here in this book . . . "

"That's wonderful, Uncle!" Verity cheered.

"No, it's not." Voshto plonked himself down in a chair. "It's taken me so long to work out the route down to the lowest level, I've grown too old to make the journey myself! My legs are way too wobbly, now."

I had to admit, Voshto moved about as quickly as a tortoise after a really nasty traffic accident.

"I'm sorry, Uncle." Verity looked sad. "I should have visited you sooner."

"Don't fret, my dear. I've booked into the Monster Rest Home for Slightly Loopy Scientists up on Level One. I'll be with others like me in happier surroundings. It will be most stimulating." Voshto smiled at Verity. "So, I suppose somebody else will have to follow this map I've made, to find that gem." His three eyes shone through his glasses. "Think of it! It'll be the ultimate discovery – and solve your human friend's little problem."

"Of course! Bob-ob-ob will be able to wish himself and his home back up above where everything's good again!" Verity gave me an encouraging smile. "Won't that be brilliant, Bob-ob-ob? And as for me, oooooh, what will I wish for . . . ?"

"The Humamon Star Jewel is not a toy, young lady," Voshto warned her sternly. "If possible, I'd like you to bring it back to me for scientific study. And so I can wish for a tap that runs slimeade and a toilet that turns into a rocket ship . . ."

"Er, excuse me." I was holding a hand up. "You said this jewel is down in the lowest level where the nastiest monsters are, right? Where we'll probably be attacked and maybe killed by almost everything we meet?"

"Yes, yes, yes! What an adventure, eh?" Voshto smiled happily. "How I wish I were going."

"I sort of wish you were too," I confessed. My mind was still reeling; could any of this be true? A jewel that granted your heart's desire sounded like something you'd find in 86% of Disney movies. There again, this underground world of monsters had sprung from somewhere, and if I didn't at least *try* to find the gem, what else would I do?

What else *could* I do?

"All right." With a sigh I held my hand out for the notebook. "Let's find this star thing."

"Hmm," said Voshto, "eager now, aren't you?"

"No," I assured him.

"Are you CERTAIN the human came here by chance, Verity?" Voshto clutched the notepad to his chest. "You're sure he's not being controlled by a ZOOLOOB?"

"A who-loob?" I said blankly.

"One of those floaty invisible brain things, you mean?" Verity shook her head. "Nahhhh. He's legit, Unc. I know it."

"We'd best be sure," said Voshto. "They can be seen when they're wet, so . . ." Suddenly he grabbed a bucket and emptied the stinky contents all over my head.

"What the flip—?" I spluttered, dripping wet.

"Ah, yes. No zooloobs on him, then." Voshto smiled.

Hang on a sec, I thought, *floaty invisible brain things?*

With a shudder, I remembered the old sci-fi film *Fiend Without A Face*. It told a tale of monsters that looked like brains-with-wiggly-spinal-cords-for-tails creepily jumping about the place. The idea that such things could be REAL here filled me with all kinds of 'UGH!'

"Well," I said, "I'm just glad that bucket of smelly water didn't come from the toilet."

"Er, yes. Isn't that, um, lucky." Voshto looked shifty. "Sorry to splash you. I had to be sure you weren't being controlled by a wicked monster who'd managed to find out about my discoveries." Voshto shook his head, and solemnly surrendered his notebook to Verity. "Now, do be careful, my child. Don't draw any attention to yourselves."

I frowned. "What do we say if anyone asks where we're going?"

"THIS!" The door was kicked open from the outside – to reveal Zola standing dramatically in the doorway, wearing a long brown raincoat, a rucksack on her back, shades in place and her snakes peeping out through an old, brown trilby hat. "Tell them you're travelling down through the levels cos you've caught an escaped gorgon and you're delivering her to her shamed and angry family."

She smiled at Verity and gestured to the notepad that held our quest. "See, I want to come with you."

"Zola!" Voshto bustled about trying to hide his papers. "Oooh, you naughty gorgon, snooping about, listening at the keyhole . . ."

"I've always known you were up to something special in here," she said firmly. "And I want to help find that jewel."

"And we all know why, don't we?" said Verity, tucking the notepad inside her toga. "You want to take it for yourself and wish for your heart's desire."

"I only want to borrow it to make one wish," said Zola simply. "I want to be a famous artist with my own great gallery, loved and respected by all. Then the other gorgons will let me go back home if I like, and I won't have to wait tables for that horrible mob downstairs."

"Well, I'm sorry," said Verity, not sounding very sorry. "My uncle found out where the jewel is, and this quest is family business." She glanced at me. "And, er, human boy business."

But at that moment I was all set to do my business in my pants. Movement through the grimy window had grabbed my attention. "Killgrotty and his greenie goons," I gasped.

"They're heading this way!"

Leaning heavily on his cane, Voshto came to see. "The Monster Army – here?!"

"I'm guessing they're not just here for the beer," said Zola.

"They're after Bob-ob-ob and me," said Verity. "What are we going to do?"

I looked helplessly at Voshto – but it was Zola who answered our question. Without a word she pulled off her hat, pushed open the dirty window and leaped right through it. Her snakes whirled their heads about like propellers to slow her down, and her raincoat puffed out like a peculiar parachute. She landed with unexpected grace right in front of Killgrotty and his guards.

"**Oi!**" Killgrotty snarled, taking a step back in surprise. "Causing a small fright to a captain in the Monster Army is an offence punishable by thirty years locked up in a small cage . . . or death!"

"A small cage would cramp my style, Mr Captain, sir! As for death, well, they do say that looks can kill . . . " She whipped off her dark glasses and stared round at each monster in turn. "But *I* prefer looks that *grill!*"

And in a flash, as if by Medusa magic, Killgrotty and his platoon were suddenly stood still, steaming and sizzling, with dark, griddle-pan lines across their uniforms and their tough, monster hides.

I gaped. "She's made big, green grill-steaks out of them!"

QUITE AN ARTISTIC STATEMENT, HUH? I CALL THIS WORK 'TOASTED SOLDIERS'.

"Only for five minutes," she called up to me, "remember? Then they'll be back to normal, only even angrier. So if we're going, we'd better go now . . ."

I turned from the window in amazement. "Verity, we should totally take her along. She'll keep Killgrotty off our backs, and protect us from any other nasty monsters we meet down below."

Verity didn't look happy, but she nodded. "What about you, Uncle?" Verity looked sadly at Voshto. "Who's going to watch out for you while Zola's gone?"

"I'll just sneak away to my rest home up top." Voshto smiled hopefully. "If you're quick, you could be back in just a couple of days!"

Zola pushed over her toasted soldiers and piled them into a heap beneath Voshto's window. "Come on, you two — it's not only art, it's a soft landing!"

The smell of pan-fried monster hide turned my tum, but Verity assured me Killgrotty and co would bounce back to normal in a matter of minutes — and in fact, they did make a pretty good crash-mat for Verity and me. Things really could've been worse.

Of course, I wildly underestimated how *much* worse . . .

CHAPTER 10

GREENISH INTERLUDE

Verity, Zola and I legged it away from The Severed Arm just as quickly as we could. The quest had begun!

I had a cold ball of worry in my stomach. Well, maybe 77% worry, 19% full-on-fear, 3.99999-recurring-% indigestion and perhaps 0.00001% optimism. Knowing there was meant to be a way out of here gave me the tiniest amount of hope, but I was terrified that the hope would be taken away from me.

It's a good job I couldn't see what was happening back at The Severed Arm, as Killgrotty and his army of thugs stopped sizzling and turned back to normal.

"A gorgon," Killgrotty snarled. "I **HATE** gorgons."

"We should be stone, but we're not," said one of his guards, with brilliant insight.

"**WELL, DON'T CRY ABOUT IT!**" Killgrotty thundered. "She didn't hold us up for long. Must be a weedy gorgon. We'll crush her if she gets in our way again." He nodded grimly. "Now let's see if anyone's seen them . . ."

Killgrotty strode up to The Severed Arm's bouncer. "I'm Captain Killgrotty of the Monster Army Special Squish-Splat Fusiliers."

"**SO?**" the bouncer shouted.

"We're looking for two dangerous fugitives – a human boy and a furball. Seen them?"

The bouncer jeered. "Why should I tell **YOU?**"

"If you don't," said Killgrotty, "my troops will zap you with laser-tasers set to level ten."

"That sounds like **FUN!**" the Bouncer declared.

Killgrotty rolled his eyes and signalled to his men. Much zapping of laser-tasers and frantic cries ensued. The bouncer was sent flying into the septic pond and lay there, cross-eyed and gently steaming.

"I was right about that being fun!" he said weakly. "Anyway, yeah, them kids you was looking for came round here, but there was a big fight and . . . Well, they must've cleared off."

"Thanks for that." Tutting to himself, Killgrotty burst into the pub with his guards right behind him, laser-tasers at the ready. The rabble of rowdy monsters fell quiet and swivelled round to face Killgrotty.

"All right, you horrible lot of layabout lard-winks! I'm after the toughest monster here to do a job for me. A job that calls for strength, stamina, and unpleasant amounts of violence." Killgrotty held up a small brown pouch. "If you are successful in this mission I will give you one hundred plogoos."

"What about hogberries?" called a monster. "I like hogberries."

"Huh?" Killgrotty scowled. "Okay, I could probably throw in a couple of hogberries."

"I like sofas," said another monster. "Can I have a sofa?"

"Ooooooh, I'd like a nice set of steak knives—"

"**SHUT UP!**" Killgrotty roared. "Who among you is the toughest and roughest of all?"

"Me!" came a high-pitched squeak, as a small rodent monster pushed through the crowd and hopped onto a table. He looked like a rat who'd been inflated with a bike pump. "I am the greatest! The meanest! The worst ever!"

With a sigh, Killgrotty pulled out an atom-masher pistol and fired it at the rodent.

"OOOOOOOOOH!" squealed the rat-thing, glowing yellow. He started running round and round the table, sparks and lightning flashes exploding from his body. "EEEEEEEEEEE!" Finally he leaped from the table into a pitcher of sour wine, which promptly blew up. The rodent was left wide-eyed, scorched, and about half his previous size. "Bah!" he squeaked. "Is that all you've got?" Then he fainted in a heap.

The pub remained silent.

"Anyone else think they're tough enough?" Killgrotty sneered.

A squat figure at the back of the room rose from his seat to his full, imposing height. His grubby shirt and trousers were rough and old, held together not by stitches but by the thick, dark stains that all but covered them. A grey hood hung over his head, hiding his features. But there was no hiding the huge twitching muscles in the two grey arms, nor the warts and blisters on the thick fingers gripping the whopping great axe.

Killgrotty fired his atom-masher. The huge figure glowed

93

and grunted, but did not move. At a nod from their captain, the greenies let rip with the laser-tasers too. The enormous figure shook a little, but stayed on his feet.

"Right. You've got the job." Killgrotty stopped firing. The greenies stopped too. A low buzz of excited, nervous chatter spread through The Severed Arm.

The massive figure just stood there.

"What's your name?" Killgrotty demanded.

"**Chopper**." The word fell from the figure's lips, heavy enough to crash through the floor. "**Chop-chop**." The figure raised his axe. "**Chopper CHOP**."

"I like your spirit, son." Killgrotty chuckled and put an arm around the massive monster. "Now, here's what you're gonna do for us . . ."

Like I said.

It's a good job I couldn't see what was happening back at The Severed Arm...

THE CONSEQUENCES OF THIS LITTLE CHAT ARE REALLY GOING TO LIVEN UP AN UPCOMING CHAPTER!

CHAPTER 11

IN A DARK, DARK WOOD THERE WAS— WHOA, WHAT IS THAT? I DON'T WANT TO KNOW! NO!!! KEEP AWAY! NOOOOOOOOOO!!!

Have you ever found yourself traipsing downhill through muck and puddles in pitch blackness with a giant hamster and a gorgon? I'm guessing probably not. In which case — congratulations!

It's not an experience I'm keen to repeat.

Voshto's map had guided us to a manhole — sorry, a monsterhole — cover in the middle of a muddy field. It was the entrance to a disused sewer, just a short fall off a broken ladder away.

This was our secret short cut down to the next level without being spotted: trudging through super-smelly, fossilised monster whoopsies in the dark. There were lots of buzzy flies around, and as Zola led the way with her shades off, she transformed them into little tiny fairylights that dropped to the floor and shone for a few minutes until her gorgon glare wore off.

"Beautiful, aren't they?" Zola sighed.

"Very useful," said Verity politely.

"Bob," Zola went on, "do you appreciate the way I'm layering colour and brightness to create intensities of light and shade?"

"Er, yeah," I said eloquently, as Zola sent another bunch of flies falling like radioactive M&Ms. "Can you transform anything, Zola?"

"Well, I've never tried turning a human being into something else." Zola popped on her shades and glanced back at me, eyebrows raised. "Your body make-up is so different to a monster's. Can you imagine what might happen?"

"I'm too busy trying *not* to imagine what I'm stepping in," I said. And, truth be told, I was feeling kind of weird now I was outnumbered by monsters on this trip. I wondered what Verity's real reasons were for risking her neck to find the jewel – to make her uncle's dream come true, or to get out of trouble with the Monster Army? Or, could it possibly be because she liked having a 'pet' human she could take for walkies? She certainly acted friendly enough. Either way, I had no choice but to follow her. If she changed her mind and went back home, I was totally stuffed.

Or would I be okay just following Zola? She was green and snaky and had claws, which I'm afraid I found a bit off-putting – but she seemed surprisingly friendly for someone who could've been a killer monster. And besides, her motives were easy to understand – she was coming along because she wanted to wish herself a happy ending, and I knew what *that* felt like.

There's no place like home, I thought dreamily, and knew I would do anything it took to get back there. Even so, this manky sewer tunnel was GROSS. "How much longer do we have to stay down here?"

I was answered with a booming clang. "OW!" yelled Zola. "By Athena's sandal, OWWWWW."

"Aha!" cried Verity, "have you just walked into a big metal hatch, Zola?"

"Ow, ow, ow, ow, YES! Ow! OW! Owwoooooooow. OWWW! Goodness Goddess, that hurt. I think two of my snakes have got mild concussion. OWW."

"Well, that's good news."

"What? How – OW! – come?"

"That hatch leads out into the Wilderness Woods." Verity

peered at the map, her dark eyes gleaming in the fly-light. "See, long ago, the muck from this old sewer came down into Level Five to help the wood grow." She pulled on a rusty wheel, which squeaked round stiffly. The hatchway slowly opened. A chink of green light entered the old sewer, and a damp, musty smell crawled into my nose.

"Here we go, then." She hopped outside. "As you humans say – GERONIMONSTERRRRRRRR!"

"We don't, actually" I complained, as Zola woozily jumped after her. Taking a deep breath, I followed them. **WHOMP!** I landed next to Zola and Verity in a large forest clearing, dimly lit by a pinky skybulb. The trees were bare and dark and gnarly, like mutant skeletons clawing at the black-mud sky high above. The ground was covered in clumps of spiky grass, like enormous house spiders turned on their backs, glowing sickly yellow. I prodded one with my foot and it left luminous stains on my trainers.

"Ugh! I feel dizzy." A couple of conked-out snakes hung down over Zola's forehead, their little scarves dangling over her shades. She gently scooped them up and smoothed them back over her head. "Think I'd better lie down for a bit." She draped herself around a tree trunk and posed in pantomime pain. "Oh! If only someone could sketch me in this position and capture my aching soul!"

"Yeah, they could call it, *Gorgon with Conked-Out Snakes Hugging Dead Tree*," I suggested.

To be honest, I was 97% more interested in the local wildlife, now we'd dropped another level. "How horrid are the monsters who live down here?" I enquired. "How long do we have before they try to splatter us?"

"Uncle Voshto chose this area because it's most deserted," Verity said, with a reassuring smile. "Most monsters around here live in high-rise caves, and they're kept in line by the Crudzilla clan."

"The who?" I asked.

"The Crudzilla clan. They're related to some massive scaly monsters that must still walk your world. Uncle V picked up transmissions of human documentaries — they smashed down cities, ate buildings, that sort of stuff. DinoBeasts."

"DinoBeasts?" I had a real 'HUH?' moment — I've seen all twenty-seven DinoBeast movies. "You mean, like . . . a sort of dinosaur-beast-monster thing?"

Verity looked at me. "Bob-ob-ob, what is this human

thing called 'dinosaur'?"

"A prehistoric monster."

"Well, I think Poppa Crudzilla's only a century old," said Verity. "But yeah, his DinoBeast relatives are, like, legends in Terra Monstra. That's why everyone down here lets the Crudzillas boss them around."

"But . . . DinoBeast isn't real!" I spluttered. "He's just special effects. Made up."

"Made up?" Verity tittered and looked at me fondly. "Aww, Bob-ob-ob, bless you. You're so naïve. Well, if it makes you feel happier, yes – DinoBeast is made up."

"He IS made up though."

"Fine."

"I mean it."

"So do I. He isn't real. Sure."

"Listen—"

A sudden, ghostly wail floated out from the gloom, whistling like wind about the skeletal tree branches.

I gulped. "On second thoughts, don't listen."

"You know, I'm an artist, not a travel guide." Zola opened her eyes dizzily. "But I think we want to go in the opposite direction to whatever made that noise."

"**CHOP-CHOP!**" came a weird, high-pitched voice from the tree-shadows behind us; a voice that chilled me to my deepest bits.

Zola, Verity and I all turned as one – to find an enormous, boss-eyed weirdo watching us from the other end of the clearing. He wore a black and white hoop top that barely contained his belly, and grey leggings that sagged in unpleasant places. His scary face looked like it had been soaked in yellow goo, but scarier still was the enormous axe he held in one hand, and the wooden club he held in the other.

I stared, transfixed with terror. "What the flip is that?"

Verity looked at least 62% more frightened than I had ever seen her. "L-l-l-looks like a jollywobble."

"It doesn't look very jolly to me," I hissed back. "It's got an axe."

"Most jollywobbles are lumberjacks." She stayed frozen as still as one of Zola's should-be-statues. "The axe is for c-c-c-cutting down trees."

"Seriously?"

"Abso-nibblin'-deffo." Verity swallowed hard. "It's that club he's holding you have to worry about. They clobber you till your bones go wobbly and you end up a living jelly."

The jollywobble pointed to himself. "**Chopper**."

Then he pointed at me and Verity. "**CHOP Chopper, chop-chop!**"

"You're quite the poet, Chopper." Zola struggled up and pulled off her shades. "So — let's see how you fare/With the terrible stare/Of the gorgon's glare!"

The Chopper looked at her. And went on looking. But nothing happened to him.

"By the pimples of Homer! Not enough snake-strength!" Zola shook her head, her sleeping serpents flopping back and forth. "He's too tough to transform!"

I groaned. "What do we do now?"

Zola looked thoughtful. "Perhaps we could try to express our feelings of fear through an interpretive dance or—"

"Not now, Zola!" I looked at Verity, who had started to shake. "Verity, got any plans, or—?"

"**CHOP! CHOP!**"

With a loopy laugh, the Chopper raised his weapons and charged towards us.

CHAPTER 12

RUN!
RUN FOR YOUR
LIIIIIIIIIIIIIIVES!

"Zola, hide!" I shouted, then yelled in Verity's ear: "RUN!"

Verity's eyes glinted green, just as they had before she'd tackled Killgrotty up on Level One. Only this time she scurried away into the forest on all fours, super-fast.

"Wait for me!" I put on a spurt of speed. I glanced back to find the Chopper was still coming right for me.

Panicking, I tried to follow the crashing of branches and footfalls as Verity ran on. But the smashing, swiping, clattering pursuit of the Chopper was growing louder in my ears as he sprinted after us like something from my worst nightmares . . .

104

With a shock, I realised: *the Chopper's got to be around 24% faster than I am. He's going to outrun me.*

What could I do?

I paused in a small clearing, panting for breath. There was nothing ahead but the dark, skinny trees and their gnarled branches.

With sudden inspiration, I hurled myself at the thickest tree I could see and began to climb, shinning up as quickly as I could. When I reached the highest of the thick branches, maybe ten metres above the ground, I clung on to the old, dead wood, trying to calm my breathing, desperate not to give myself away.

The Chopper came lumbering down below. But he didn't glance upward, or round and about. He kept crashing onwards through the old, dead vegetation and was soon lost from my sight.

I'd given the jollywobble the slip!

Unable to believe my luck, I held onto my branch like a three-toed sloth in a particularly boring wildlife documentary. The forest was silent now. Where was Verity? Did I dare to climb down and go looking for her? Should I head back to see if Zola was okay?

Forget about the documentary — I was up to my neck in monster movie territory. And I imagined the credits of my personal monster movie might carry a disclaimer:

NO HUMANS WERE HARMED
IN THE MAKING OF THIS
MOTION PICTURE. EXCEPT FOR
BOB BEE, OF COURSE. WE
HURT HIM REALLY BAD! AND
ALL HIS FRIENDS! AFTER WE
STOLE HIS HOUSE AND
TRASHED IT AND NARROWLY
MISSED SNATCHING HIS
BABYSITTER TOO, THAT IS.

Suddenly – "**Chop! Choppy-Chop!**"

The chilling Chopper was back. He pushed out of the dead, crackly trees and stood looking around. I held my breath. To be honest it felt more like my breath was holding me, dead tight around my whole body, so tight I really couldn't budge.

Maybe he won't look up and see me, I thought.

The Chopper immediately looked up and saw me. "Chop-Chop!" he called. "**Chopper chop!**"

"Leave me alone!" I howled.

"**Choppy!**" The Chopper raised his axe and swung it. ***THUNK!*** The axe-blade bit deep into the tree. A weird vibration shook through the trunk and I gripped on more tightly. ***WOINNNG!*** He bashed the bark with the mallet, and it wobbled alarmingly.

I felt the trunk shake a little more with each sharp

THUNK! and wobbly **whack!** I dangled helplessly high above the forest floor; it was as if the old branch was weighed down with a big Bob fruit – a fruit ripe to be plucked and squished . . .

"Please, noooooooooo!" I yelled. My heart was thumping so hard and fast in my chest it felt more like a motor roaring away inside. I could almost hear the fierce thrum . . .

Then I realised: there was no 'almost' about it – deep, whirring thunder was growing louder in my ears.

Looking up, I thought I must be going fruit-loops. A very different kind of chopper had swept into view overhead! Big, rusty and battered like most vehicles in Terra Monstra, a strange helicopter gleamed in the dim bulb-light, its spinning rotors shifting dust from the solid dirt sky.

Suddenly, the copter dipped and tilted to one side, and the spinning rotors sliced through the dead branches of the neighbouring tree. A storm of splinters tore through the air, narrowly missing me . . .

. . . and whacking right into the Chopper! With a wail, he turned and dropped his axe and his mallet, as his butt was peppered with a thousand thorny bullets.

Yelping and hopping about with pain, the Chopper ran blindly into a tree and conked his forehead. **FLOMP!** He collapsed and banged the back of his head on his own mallet. **WOINGGGG!** His head rang like a wobbly bell, and he lay still.

But there was no time for triumph. The tree was ready to fall; the Chopper had done most of his wobbly work, and the gale whipped up by the helicopter was finishing it off . . .

"WHOAAAAAAA!" As the tree and I began to lose the argument with gravity, the helicopter dipped and darted towards us. For a horrid moment, I fell – then grabbed hold of one of the landing skids at the copter's base. The tree wasn't so lucky – it hit the ground in an explosion of dust and dead wood, while I dangled above it like an action hero...

... for at least three seconds – before I lost my grip on the landing skid and dropped down to earth.

They say a cat always lands on its feet. Good for the cat, stupid show-off! Not being a cat, I landed on my bum in a pile of mud and twigs, while the copter touched down in a small clearing close by.

My heart beat harder as a creepy claw pushed out from the copter's cockpit — and the owner of that claw soon followed.

CHAPTER 13

BEHOLD... CRUDZILLÄ! ALFIE CRUDZILLÄ.

I stared at the creature before me.

And who could blame me?

It looked as if a child had fallen in a monster dressing-up box and made several bad decisions. My first thought was that a yellow dinosaur onesie had collided with a giant prawn: there were two floppy tails, two spiky claw-things, one much larger than the other, while the head of the 'monster' was lolling to one side. A big eye and a small eye — both orange — fixed on me.

113

The figure's rubbery jaws, complete with rubbery teeth, began to flap open and closed. "Er . . . hey, man," came a surprisingly American-sounding voice. "Where'd you spring from? You're human, aren't you? You don't live in the caves."

"Er, no," I agreed.

"And you're not going to . . .?" He mimed shooting stuff out of his nose.

"Toxic waste? I promise you, I couldn't if I wanted to."

"Oh. Well, in that case . . . **I'M DOWN WITH THE BOOM!**" He gave a big rubbery grin. "How about you, man? You down with the boom?"

"I'm . . . down on the ground?"

"Yeah, but are you down with the **BOOM**?"

"Er, would you like me to be?" I climbed warily to my feet. "What IS the 'boom'?"

"What's the boom? Awwww, c'mon, man. The boom is . . ." Rubber-jaws stood there, contemplating. "Uh, actually, I have no idea what the boom is. But I'm down with it, man! See, it's kind of my catchphrase."

I was beginning to think I had cracked up. "You . . . have a catchphrase?"

"C'mon, you're a human, you know this stuff! I'm Alfie Crudzilla, stand-up comedian, see? Or I want to be a stand-up comedian, anyway." He smiled. "There used to be quite a few monster stand-ups on the upper levels, long time back. Nowadays, monsters are meaner. The laughter kind of stopped. And I say it's time for a comeback!" He shrugged. "Anyway, all the great comics had a catchphrase. Did you ever catch Honky Tooth-Blammer's act? He'd always say,

'HEY, HEY, HEY, NICE TO DESTROY YOU!'
What a scream! From his audiences I mean, when he ate
them."

"Right," I said, glancing around. "Well, thanks for the
rescue, but I've got a friend to find—"

"Big Jock McDeathsaw, he was another big star. What did
he used to say when he came on stage? 'I'M GONNA KILL
YOU!' Priceless, man. So, I'm **DOWN WITH
THE BOOM**." Alfie sighed. "Trouble is, my sisters
prefer knock-down to stand-up. So whenever I try to do my
act, they knock down my audience. Which normally means,
they flatten our mom."

I laughed despite myself. "Hey, that's quite funny."

"I was being serious, man." Alfie glared at me. "See, Pop
and my sisters want me to follow them into the family
business of acting tough to get cash out of the monsters
round here. Trouble is, I'm no good. They can grow super-
big and tall like the real DinoBeast and terrify everybody,
and, well, I can't."

"Really?" I heard Zola's voice, and saw her peeping around
a branch, while her recovered snakes peeped out from
behind a twig just above it. "Good."

"Zola!" I ran over to join her. "You're all right?"

"Bit of a headache still." She looked cross. "The Chopper ignored me. He just wasn't interested! Honestly, everyone's a critic!"

"Tell me about it," Alfie said with feeling. "That jollywobble who was after you. He *wrecked* my act at The Severed Arm's Bring-Your-Own-Coffin Talent Night – laughing at the wrong bits, attacking members of the audience with his mallet . . . I was happy to fill his butt with splinters." He shook his head. "Sheesh, man, I wish I could cheer up these lower levels a little. Make things a bit better, you know? I wish someone would give me the chance."

"You ever hear of the Humamon Star Jewel?" Zola said brightly.

I frowned. Wasn't our quest meant to be secret?

"This brilliant old professor told us where it is," she went on, "and we're on an artistically-fulfilling quest to fetch it."

Alfie's mouth flapped open. "You mean, that old jewel legend is real?"

"Totally! And if you hold that jewel, it will grant your heart's desires. It's going to make me a famous artist, so I'll win the respect of all the gorgons who kicked me out of town!"

"Seriously?" Alfie high-fived her with his big pincer. "That's down with the **BOOM**, man! Uh, I mean, lady. Uh, gorgon. You think maybe I could help you find it and make a wish too?"

"Well, I'm not sure," I said. "We should really get going. Thanks for saving my life, Alfie, but we've got to find our friend Verity."

"She's the one with the map of how to find the Star Jewel," Zola put in.

"Zola," I hissed, "it's meant to be a secret!"

"But he's got a helicopter!" Zola beamed. "He could help us find Verity! We can't get anywhere without her."

I had to accept, this was a good point well made.

"Sure, you can ride in the copter with me if you like, see if you can spot her." Alfie Crudzilla slapped us heartily on the backs. "I won't charge you . . . but I might try out a few new jokes!"

"Yes, please!" Zola shook hands too (while her snakes gave little bows and curtseys). "It's always nice to meet a fellow creative type. But what were you even doing in a helicopter when, er, there isn't that much sky around here?"

"I'm just scaring up the cave dwellers to pay their rent,"

Alfie explained. "Since I can't fight or flatten anybody, my sisters say it's the only thing I'm good for." He turned and unfolded a crumpled banner hanging from the rear of the copter; with the vehicle in flight, it clearly trailed out behind. The banner read:

"Interesting," said Zola, as her snakes sized up the sign. "I like the deliberate use of crude, primitive letters and that rich shade of red."

"That's Poppa's best handwriting," said Alfie, ushering us into the cramped confines of the copter. "He wrote it in the blood of some dude who couldn't pay his rent – so I guess it's actually a *poor* shade of red. Heh! Get it?"

I grimaced as I sat down in a metal chair. "That's kind of mean."

"Don't sweat it, man — I was just kidding. It's really squashed berry juice."

"Oh." I nodded. "That's all right then."

"Berries squashed by someone who couldn't pay his rent so he got thrown off a building!" Alfie shook a claw. "Boom! I'm down with it! No, no, he wasn't really thrown off a building."

"Good," I said, relieved.

"He had a ten-ton weight dropped on him instead. **BOOM!** Or did he? Ha ha! No, he didn't. Probably! Heh." Alfie climbed into the pilot's seat and hit the starter, and the rotors started to turn. "I think you'll find I'm a natural wit!"

"Wit?" Zola smiled as she sat beside me. "You missed off the 'T' at the beginning."

"Ooh, that gag's not bad, man! Mind if I use that?"

Alfie's claws gripped the control stick and the whirlybird soared into the air. My stomach lurched as I looked down on the forest far below. Looking up, I could see that a long way ahead the woods ended, making way for a burnt-orange cliff-face, sinister caves and scrubby open spaces.

"That's where everyone on this level lives," said Alfie.

"I'd better get flashing the banner so they get their cash ready. My sisters will be visiting them any time now."

"Hey! I see something moving down there." Zola pointed out a flash of grey in the dark of the undergrowth. "The Chopper's back on his feet."

"And running," I realised, as we zoomed overhead. "Like he's chasing after . . . uh-oh!"

There, scampering for her life away from the Chopper, heading for the forest's edge... was Verity.

"HEY!" I bellowed over the noise of the copter. "Verity, it's us!" I was 71% glad to find she was okay, 27% alarmed to find she soon might not be, and around 2% airsick. But Verity seemed 100% set on shifting her tail through the trees; despite the racket over her head, she didn't look up. "I guess she must be in shock."

Zola gripped my arm with her claws and pointed. "By Hercules' pants, she's going to get one."

I followed her finger, and gasped to see a familiar gang of green gargoyles standing guard at the perimeter of the woods.

Killgrotty and his greenie-gang were back.

CHAPTER 14

CAUGHT BETWEEN THE DEVIL AND THE DEEP BLUE SEA. OR RATHER, BETWEEN KILLGROTTY AND A BUNCH OF OTHER BAD STUFF.

I turned to Zola. "Think it's a coincidence that the Chopper's driving her towards Killgrotty? Alfie said he'd seen the Chopper at The Severed Arm."

"Not for a date, or anything," Alfie said quickly.

"Killgrotty could have stopped off there and recruited that jollywobble to help him get you," Zola agreed, as her snakes hissed and nodded. "Well, if Verity doesn't stop running blind soon, his plan will work – she's going to end up charging right into his arms!"

"He doesn't look the type you'd wanna hug for long," said Alfie. "I'll go in low, see if we can make her snap out of it."

My tummy turned as Alfie took the copter down sharply. "Whoaaaaaaaa!"

"Relax, man!" Alfie clung to the control stick with both claws. "I've only crashed this thing four times, and none of them were fatal. Well, not to me, anyway!"

We almost scraped the skeletal treetops as we passed. Trying not to fall out through the window I shouted down at Verity: "Stop! You're running straight for—"

I broke off as blasts of sizzling green slime smacked into the helicopter right beside my head. Killgrotty's guards had opened fire, trying to bring us down.

"Take her up!" I yelled. "We're under attack!"

A blast of green slop washed over the window, blinding us. "Whoa! We'd better split." Alfie turned the copter in a tight circle and steered upwards in an erratic zigzag. "Sorry, guys. I tried to help, but I couldn't."

I stared at him. "You can't give up!"

"Course I can. It's the only thing I'm good at." He sighed. "Besides, my sisters will hit the roof if I trash another copter."

"We'll all hit the roof if you go up too high." Zola's snakes were standing on end. "I'm sure we'd make artistic stains, but even so."

"Hey, I'm meant to be the comedian round here!" Alfie complained – and then he groaned. "Aww, no. Of all the luck! There are my sisters now."

"Where?" Dizzily, Zola peered out at the caves and wasteland. "I don't see anyone—EEEK!"

Two huge, prehistoric dinosaur types had shot up from the ground. I could see the resemblance to DinoBeast – for about 0.023 seconds, before I hid my face in my hands and gibbered like a loon.

There was a **CLANG** and a lurch as one of the giant monsters caught the copter's landing skids in her claws and leered through the slimy windscreen. "What're you up to, doofus-face?"

"Bob, I think she's talking to you," Zola whispered.

"She means Alfie!" I hissed back, as the copter rocked in the monster's grip. "Look, can't you zap her with your gorgon glare?"

"I'm an artist, not a painter and decorator!" Zola retorted. "Honestly, I really couldn't turn THAT massive monster into anything. And anyway, the other one would squash us flat!"

"Uh, hi, sis," said Alfie. "I just came to tell you . . . there's this bunch of tough monsters at the west end of the forest and they say they're taking over our patch cos the Crudzillas are a bunch of wimps."

I opened my eyes a fraction, just as Big Sis's eyes narrowed to fiery slits.

"They say **WHAT?**" She turned her head and huge gouts of flame burst from her jaws. "**I'LL STOMP THEM INTO MUSH!**" Releasing the helicopter she lumbered away in the style of a man in a rubber suit trashing a model set for movie cameras — only horribly real.

"Nice one, Alfie!" I clapped him on the shoulder. "I wouldn't want to be in Killgrotty's shoes now."

"Me neither. Can you imagine how bad his feet must smell?" Alfie grinned. "First rule of stand-up comedy, man — you gotta be fast."

"Let's try to grab Verity," I said. "If we can land long enough to lift her up into the air with us ..."

We raced past the giant reptilian head of Big Sis One and back over the forest. There was the Chopper, waving his mallet, gaining on Verity who was still running, and drawing closer and closer to Killgrotty and co.

But it was a sure bet that Big Sis One would reach them first.

The greenies looked up as the scary shadow of Big Sis One fell over the forest's edge. "Try to muscle in on our patch, will ya? GROAARRRRRRRRR!" she roared, trampling trees as she stamped down with her enormous scaly foot. The impact shook Killgrotty and his entire platoon to their knees, and the tremors sent the Chopper and Verity sprawling too. Killgrotty pulled out a bigger weapon from a backpack and blasted jagged green crackles of energy into Big Sis One.

"**ARRGH!**" She threw back her head with anger, and almost toasted us with a fresh burst of flames from the back of her throat. Alfie yanked hard on the control stick and we swerved from the fire so fast that I almost tumbled out through the window. Zola's snakes grabbed my top with their little jaws, and, with their owner's help, managed to hold me back.

Thanks," I told the gorgon. "I thought I was going to fall!"

"It's not the fall you have to worry about," said Alfie, "it's that sudden stop at the end of it!"

"**SISSSSSS!**" thundered Big Sis One. "Give me a claw over here, will ya?"

"Things are going to get messy." Alfie sent the copter plummeting towards the treetops. "Time to get

DOWN WITH THE BOOOOOOOOM!"

My heart was left up in the air as we plunged towards the heavy branches. I screwed up my eyes and tensed my body, ready for a crash landing . . .

But the crash didn't come. Incredulous, I opened my eyes to find we were hovering above the ground in a small clearing – Alfie must've spotted it from the air. Suddenly, a high-speed hamster-thing came haring into sight, on a collision course!

"Verity!" I cried. "Slow down, you're going to—"

WHAM! She ran face-first into one of the landing skids. I grabbed hold of a paw before she could slump to the ground, and Zola grabbed hold of me to stop me falling out again.

Then the Chopper burst into the clearing, hot on Verity's paws, waving his axe.

"Hold on!" Alfie swung the copter round through three hundred and sixty degrees and – **WHUMP!** – the tail rotor smashed into the Chopper's back, knocking him to the ground. "How's **THAT** for a punchline?"

"Technically, you didn't punch him," Zola pointed out. "I'm not sure the joke works."

"Could we try and stay focused, please?" I called, still half outside, clinging on to poor, dazed Verity. "We've got to get her inside the helicopter!"

The landscape shook as heavy reptilian feet crashed around close by. Slime splattered, energy blasts crackled and trees burst into flame or were knocked down around us as Alfie's big (or frankly, ENORMOUS) sisters fought the might of the Monster Army.

Hang on, I thought. *Killgrotty's missing. Shouldn't he be leading the fight? Where's he gone?*

But there was no time to worry about Killgrotty now.

"Look out!" Zola cried, pointing to the Chopper, who was back on his feet. He swung his axe at the side of the copter, drawing sparks from the metal. Alfie spun us round again, tangling the Chopper up in Alfie's banner behind. The jollywobble struggled, making the copter pitch like crazy.

Then, over the roar of the rotors I could hear the fierce crackle of energy blasts and the angry roar of a Big Sis: **"PUNY GREEN GOOPERS, I'M GONNA BELLY-FLOP ON TOP OF YOU!"**

"Uh-oh," Alfie yelled. "Big Sister incoming. That belly of hers will take out this part of the forest – we have to take off **NOW!**"

Unfortunately, the Chopper had other ideas – and a tight hold on the banner's towrope. He wouldn't let us go.

Verity's eyes flickered open – and widened with fear as she scrabbled for a better grip on the landing skid. "What the—?"

"Keep holding on!" I yelled over the din.

"To what, my sanity?" Verity panted. "I'm exhausted, I'm hanging from a helicopter and I seem to be flashing my pants to a crazed, axe-wielding, mallet-swinging jollywobble!"

"And on top of that, a giant Crudzilla is about to start an earthquake!" I yelled. "Alfie, we've got to break loose right now!"

"Allow me!" Verity kicked out with her foot-claws and sliced through the rope. **RRRIIIIPPPPPP!** The Chopper fell back onto his splinter-filled bum.

"Whoa!" Alfie struggled with the control stick as we rose up into the air. "The engine's really straining. Your furry friend on the skid must be heavier than she looks!"

"Cheek!" Verity squeaked.

"But I'm guessing your sister is *just* as heavy as she looks," I said, fascinated as a blur of orange scales flashed past the window. **KA-BRUMMMMMMMMMM!** – the Chopper, several greenies and a fair-sized portion of Wilderness Woods were squashed flat by the giant, nosediving she-monster.

As the shockwaves rumbled through the forest below, I felt a tidal wave of relief wash over me. "Whew! That's taken care of our pursuers, then."

"Er, not quite!" Verity squeaked. Still hanging onto the left skid, she was staring in horror at the right skid.

Where a familiar, grimacing green figure was dangling outside, glaring up at me.

Killgrotty had escaped the giant Crudzillas. . . by grabbing a free ride with us!

CHAPTER 15

SWAMPED!

I watched, whimpering, as Killgrotty stared up at me from the landing skid. "You revolting human," he growled, "you've got to be stopped!"

Zola leaned over, pulled off her shades and tried to gorgon-glare at him, but Killgrotty looked away quickly.

"Hey, man, I don't pick up hitchhikers!" Alfie took the copter higher into the air, weaving from side to side. "You get me?"

"Careful!" I warned him. "You'll shake off Verity too!"

"Let the fluff-ball go!" I heard Killgrotty shout. "You can't use her like this!"

"Huh?" I leaned out the window, but could only see his

big green fists holding on to the skid. "Captain, seriously, I'm not using Verity like anything!"

"You want to use the Star Jewel to grant your evil wishes," Killgrotty was saying. "You'll bring disaster down on us all. Is it worth it? **IS IT?**"

"What are you on about?" I cried. "I just want to go home!"

"Release her!" Killgrotty snarled. "You landed yourself here, and you'll never get out."

"Hey, I just had an idea," Alfie piped up. "A real bulb-over-the-head moment."

Looking up, I realised our pilot was speaking literally – he was steering the copter straight for the skybulb! It was bigger than I'd thought – the size of a caravan at least, and fizzing with pinky-white light.

"OOOOH!" Zola squealed, and her snakes looked delighted. "Goddess above, what an artistic statement THIS is going to be!"

It was too late to shout any warnings, too late to do anything – even close my eyes. Alfie turned the copter at the last moment so that the right landing skid smashed into the skybulb – with Killgrotty still holding on.

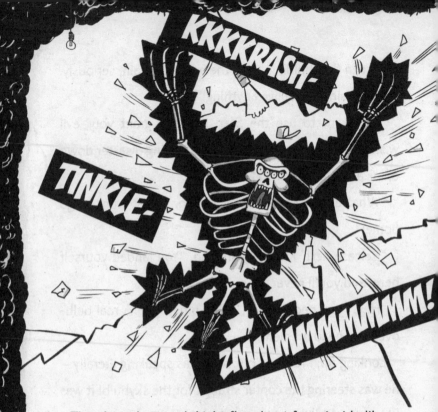

KKKKRASH-

TINKLE-

ZMMMMMMMMMM!

The glass shattered. Light flared out from inside like a caged creature suddenly released. Killgrotty was knocked from the skid and held suspended: zapped, blapped and eerie-fied in the power-flow while we flew on, with Verity still somehow clinging to the other skid. The spooky glow sputtered and faded, leaving darkness.

"I guess we made *light* work of Killgrotty, huh?" quipped Alfie, holding up a pincer. "Oh, yeah! I'm **DOWN WITH THE BOOM!**"

"Ooooh, Alfie!" Zola was quivering. "That was, like, radical sky theatre!"

"You've killed him!" I cried in shock.

"Nah." Shaking his head, Alfie flicked on the copter's headlamps and circled back towards the wreckage. "Look!"

With a mix of fear and admiration, I saw that Killgrotty had managed to grip hold of the filament inside the shattered skybulb. Scorched, singed and smoking, the soldier dangled there grimly as Alfie circled round for another view.

"**YOU'RE FOR IT NOW!**" Killgrotty shouted. "Breaking skybulbs is punishable by the death of a thousand splats."

"Don't get heavy, man!" Alfie saluted. "You should get **LIGHT!** Get it?"

Letting go with one hand, Killgrotty drew a gun from his hip holster. "I'll show you heavy!"

"No," said Zola. "I'll show you!" She glared at the soldier through the window. The tough monster had no time to look away.

And in a blink and a blur, Killgrotty and his gun were

transformed into scrap-metal, the same colour and texture as the copter itself, bashed about, bolted together – but also festooned with flowers. He plunged from the roof like a highly decorative meteor, soon swallowed by darkness.

"Well, whaddyaknow!" Alfie beamed. "He's gone down with the **BLOOM!**"

"I call that still life, *Heavy Petal*." Zola put on her shades and smiled happily. "Did it make your heart sing, artsy human boy? Did it?"

"Hey!" came a weak squeak from outside. "Anyone interested in helping out a half-flattened furry thing?"

"Verity! Flip, I forgot about you . . ." I leaned out into the darkness, felt for a furry arm, found it. With Zola's help, I hauled in the hamster-monster. She lay quivering on the floor, looking up at us, a faint green glow in her eyes, just as when she'd fought Killgrotty and his goons up on Level One.

"It's okay," I told her. "It's over now."

"Over?" Verity smiled weakly up at me. "Abso-nibblin'- no way! After tonight's little show the Monster Army will chuck everything at us. They'll do anything to stop us now! We've **GOT** to find the Star Jewel as quickly as possible."

Confused cries and shouts were floating out from the

darkened caves and cliffs below.

"Who turned out the lights?"

"Is there a power cut?"

"DOES THIS MEAN WE CAN GET MONEY OFF THE RENT?"

"Did that dur-brain in the helicopter have something to do with this?"

"I'll crush him!"

"I'll splatter him!"

"I'll dip him in batter and eat him raw!"

"Um, something tells me I'd better get out of here till the heat is off a little," said Alfie. "I have a request. Well, it's re: your quest. Zola mentioned you're all looking for the Star Jewel. Can I come with?"

"Sure! You just earned it, pilot boy!" Verity winked at him. "And as a reward, when we find the jewel, you can use it to wish for your heart's desire. How cool is that?"

"That's **(OOOOO-OOOOO-OOOOL**, man!" Alfie punched the air with his little pincer. "Okay! Which way? Which way?"

Verity pulled her uncle's crumpled notes from inside her toga. "Let me see . . ."

I was slightly surprised at how easily Verity had let Alfie

join our little band, but then he had proved himself to be good in a tight spot, just like Zola, and his copter could keep us clear of the nasty, destructive monsters below.

"I'm glad that the skybulb's gone out," Verity murmured, "because now, no one will see us sinking and try to follow us."

"Sinking?" My heart was doing much the same. "We're in a helicopter! What do you mean, sinking?"

"I mean that according to the map, we're going to have to touch down in the porridge swamps to the west." The green glint had left her eyes now – they fixed on me, wide and black. "Of course, it'll seem like we're sinking to our deaths as the slop slips over us, buried forever in grey lumpy sludge. But Uncle says there's a big crack in the ground below. All we have to do is get through it, and we'll be in the next level!"

"Is that all?" I groaned. "Can't we just go there by nogglodon?"

"That's 'nogg*looooo*don'."

"Stop that."

"Anyway, Killgrotty will have all those exits covered, remember?" Verity went on. "We have to take the road less travelled."

"Or the swamp less died in," Alfie suggested.

"Oh, a whole lot of folk have died in it," Zola informed us cheerily. "But Verity's right. It's very wise to sneak into Level Six — it isn't safe. It's the extreme opposite of safe."

I looked at her, uneasy. "Sounds as if you know a lot about it."

"I do. Level Six is where I'm from," Zola revealed. "I've heard of this back way in. We'll plop out in Death-Eye Canyon in the gorgon capital of Gorgopolis — one of the deadliest spots in all Terra Monstra!"

No one spoke for a little while.

"Well," said Alfie in a small voice, "maybe being crushed to a pulp by my gigantic killer sister won't be so bad after all! How about I just drop you off near the swamps and—"

"Awww, c'mon! It'll be a hundred times harder without you." Verity put an arm around Alfie and licked his cheek. "Anyway, we'll be all right. No risk, no frisk! Where's your spirit of adventure?"

"I think mine's been exorcised," I said miserably. Killgrotty was so wrong! I wasn't using Verity. It seemed that, if anything, she was using us!

But I was glad she was still on my side after all she'd been through since I pitched up here. To get the jewel, and to get out of Monsterland . . . how could I do it without her?

I reached over and gave her paw a squeeze. She smiled back at me happily.

But Zola did not look happy at all.

An hour later, Alfie brought the helicopter low over the porridge swamp – which was just as weird and unpleasant as it sounded. The worst thing was the smell, which was more like an over-excited skunk setting off stink bombs in a rotten-egg-and-cabbage factory.

Well, I say that was the worst thing. But then a few minutes later we were slowly descending towards that evil-stinking mire. In the helicopter's headlights I watched it surge, bubble and plop. It seemed almost . . . hungry.

I looked at Zola. She had hardly spoken the whole journey, staring at the map through her shades. "You sure this is the right spot?"

She nodded. "This is it, all right."

Suddenly we stopped going down. "I . . . I can't do this!" Alfie cried. "This is crazy, man! I mean, no magic wish is worth getting suffocated by porridge for. Am I right?"

"Abso-nibblin'-*no-you're not!*" Verity tipped him out of

the pilot's seat and pushed up on the control stick. With a lurch and a jolt and a **SQUELCH**, we swooped down into the sick-smelling swamp of monster porridge.

Alfie made a high-pitched squeaky noise. "What have you done?"

"Speeded things up a little," said Verity, switching off the engines: the rotors sighed to a stop, and all was sinister silence. "Killgrotty won't have stayed as metal for long – and he'll be jumping mad, coming after us with everything he's got, trying to stop us reaching the Star Jewel. Every second counts."

"Especially when you're running out of them," I agreed dismally. Already the thick, slurping porridge was up against the windows. We were sinking . . . sliding. . . .

CLAUSTROPHOBIAAAAAAAAAAAAAAAAA!

"Maybe you should switch on the rotors again," I said, "we could rise back out of here?"

"Too late," Zola whispered. The gloop was almost at the top of the windows now. Disgusting **SQUELCH-SQUERCH-SCHLURRRRP** sounds were growing louder all around us. The headlights had been swallowed; I couldn't see anything at all through the windows, the darkness of the swamp-muck was absolute. The helicopter's hull creaked and groaned as the porridge pressure increased, as the sucking, slurping noises got louder, deeper and more revolting. The faint glow of the copter's controls gave our only light.

"How does this crack in the bottom of the swamp even work?" cried Alfie. "If it's real, what stops the porridge in the swamp from seeping out of it?"

"I don't know," Verity admitted. "But Uncle Voshto is an expert. If he says it's the best way in, it's the best way in."

GLOPP! The porridge closed over us. An oaty silence settled.

"We're completely under the swamp," Alfie whispered.

"How do we even find this crack in the bottom?" I asked Verity.

A deep, growling, horrible noise echoed all around us.

Zola looked grave. "Sounds as if something has found us!"

Alfie flicked a switch and the headlights grew brighter, spilling just a little light through the cockpit windows. I saw the sluggish swirl of gloop draining away into a dark hole.

A dark hole with a fat red tongue lolling in its centre.

A dark hole framed by huge, tombstone teeth.

"There's something horrible down here," I realised. "It's going to swallow us whole!"

CHAPTER 16

CREATURE
DISCOMFORTS

"Help! Help!" I wanted to run around in a panic, but the cockpit was so squashed with four of us inside that I could hardly move. "What are we going to do?"

"We've got to get out of here!" Alfie was hammering the engine buttons, trying to restart the rotors. "I didn't sign up to be lunch for a monster."

"Don't worry, it'll be all right." Verity was totally calm, quietly licking at her fur. "I know something you don't."

"Of course!" Zola nodded, as her snakes stifled little giggles. "The reason you wanted to come here inside something."

"Less mucky that way," Verity agreed.

"What?" I demanded. "What're you on about?"

The sludgy blackness around us gave way to pink,

glistening flesh, and suddenly we were thrown about, tumbling down into unknown glistening depths.

"Noooooo!" I shouted, horrified. "We're falling down this thing's throat!"

"We have to, Bob-ob-ob!" Verity assured me. Disgusting wobbling, bobbling, fleshy walls pressed in all around. "It's the only way down to the crack."

"Huh?" Alfie looked blank. "But, the swamp is outside, and we're inside this thing ..."

Zola smiled. "It's not a crack in the bottom of the swamp. It's a crack in the bottom of this monster!"

"You mean ..." I blinked. "This crack we're going through is a *bum*-crack?"

Verity held up a page from her uncle's notes and read aloud: "*There is a vast monster in the porridge swamp that feeds on nothing but the horrid gunk all around there. Its giant bottom sits in a sinkhole like a humungous plug in the base of a bathtub. Breathing through an extra-long snorkel, I plan to sink into the monster's mouth and pass through its digestive system, finally exiting safely via the bum into a cave in Level Six.*" She looked up and grinned a broad, beaverish grin. "Since I forgot to pack an extra-long snorkel and a change of clothes, I thought maybe we could go down in this thing instead, huh?"

"When you said we'd plop out, Zola, man, I didn't realise how right you were!" Alfie clutched his rubbery stomach. "You do realise my copter's not insured for 'acts of bottom'?"

The sounds of gurgling and belly-growls grew even louder. I just hoped the thing that had swallowed us wasn't constipated.

"My monster movies were never like this," I said. "Although I guess there was the Blob in, er, *The Blob*. That was a big red amoeba from outer space that grew bigger the more people it ate."

"Eating *people?* Ugh!" Zola turned up her green nose. "I'd sooner have the porridge."

"Me too." I gave a wistful sigh. "You know, I used to be 83% certain I wanted to become a film director and make my own monster movies when I grew up. Now, I don't know."

Alfie looked at me. "So, there are other movies up top besides the ones about Cousin DinoBeast, huh?"

"They're just stories," I told him. "Humans like to make

up stories about monsters."

"Why?" wondered Verity.

"Well, cos creepy monster stories are cool."

"You like being scared?" said Zola. "You must love it here."

"No," I said with feeling. "Humans only like being scared when we know it's not real. But no one knows that monsters are really real . . . except me, now." I shook my head. "You know, it's way too much of a coincidence that I love monster movies so much and wound up here. It must be cos my family have lived on top of the leak from Terra Monstra for so long. It must've affected us. You know, like when you dream about something you've been thinking of that day? 61% of my dreams are like that."

"What's with you and percentages, Bob-ob-ob?" Verity wondered. "You seem to use them quite a lot."

She was right, of course. I use percentages maybe 40 – 50% of the time. "I don't know." I shrugged. "Everyone in my family does it. It's just a thing. Like the way you can't say nogglodon."

"Nogglo*don*."

"Leave it."

A protesting, squeaking, squelching noise started up and the copter slipped downwards. "Ugh! Alfie waved a pincer in front of his beak. "What a stink!"

TBH, I'd sooner not relive those mucky moments as we flopped out of the monster's colossal backside, but here is an artist's impression of our escape:

OTHER STINKS ARE AVAILABLE - SUCH AS *ALIENS STINK* FROM MAGIC INK PRODUCTIONS. SORRY TO INTERRUPT. BYE!

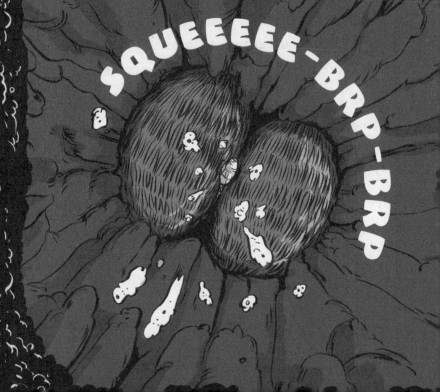

SQUEEEEE-BRP-BRP

Finally, huddled together and bracing ourselves against the sides of the cockpit – "WHOAAAAAAA!" we dropped from above in a swampy **SPLAT** – luckily, the right way round. I tried to offer a grateful word of thanks to the heavens, but of course there was a gigantic hairy butt blocking my view and I wasn't about to thank THAT for anything.

So we carefully got out of the helicopter on wobbly legs. The ground was rocky underfoot. A wild, whistling wind howled outside.

"We're in a cave," said Verity.

Alfie nodded. "A spooky cave."

"I'd better take a look and see where we are." Zola picked up a flat slate from the cave floor. "Tell you what! I'll sketch the landscape in chalks, then come back and unveil it to you during a small ceremony."

"Or we could just come with you and see for ourselves," I suggested.

"No sense of occasion, you humans." Zola looked glum and her snakes had drooped a little. "I'm just trying to put off going out there."

"Oh, it can't be as bad as all that. Can it?" Verity pushed

her paw into my hand and took a deep, shaky breath. "Come on. Let's view the view from Death-Eye Canyon."

We followed her through a cold, damp, dark tunnel, silt and sand scraping under our feet.

"I hear tourists love Gorgonopolis," said Alfie suddenly. "They come to visit – and they never leave! Ha! Ha . . . er, ha?" None of us responded. "Er, the joke is, they come here and get killed by being turned into statues so they can't leave—"

"Maybe you should cut that one from the routine," I broke in.

"Why did the gorgon cross the road?" Alfie tried again. "To kill someone by turning them to stone!"

Verity shivered. "And that one."

"My gorgon has no nose," Alfie tried again. "How does she smell? It doesn't matter, because she kills anyone within sniffing distance by turning them to—"

"Could you stop, please?" I hissed.

"Sorry, guys." Alfie sighed. "When I'm scared, I make jokes about it. It's just kind of what I do."

"Well, you're right to be scared," Zola called from ahead of us, standing on a ledge outside the cave. "Here it is.

Night-time in Death-Eye Canyon."

I joined her on the ledge, while Alfie and Verity held back in the cave-mouth, and peered into the misty, menacing gloom. A dim skybulb shone purple from a socket of rock. Drops of sharp-smelling water dripped from the stone heavens high above, falling like rain. The scree-covered slopes of the canyon were littered with strange rock formations.

Or that's what I thought at first, anyway.

Then I saw they were statues. Some new and white, some old and moss-grown, all that now stood of monsters turned to stone while climbing desperately in search of safety. One last glance over their shoulder at their sinister pursuers, and they'd been petrified in more way than one.

There were other things in the valley. Tall and thin like people in the misty shadows?

Daylight snapped on as the skybulb flicked into life, a hard, pale purple. I jumped in alarm. Yes, I could see more clearly now. Other figures standing in the canyon and crouched on the slopes . . . green skin protruding from robes and capes, with hair like nests of vipers . . . or anacondas . . . or even boa constrictors . . .

The scene was suddenly 77% scarier.

"Gorgons!" Alfie whispered, cringing in the cave mouth, pointing down into the valley. "Loads of them!" Sweat was beading on his rubbery skin, his voice was growing more and more high-pitched. "It's like a chorus line of gorgons out there! Look, see? Gorgons. **GORGONS, EVERYWHERE!**"

"Shhhh," I hissed. "They'll hear you!"

Alfie threw his head back and wailed: "**GORRRRRGOONNNNNNS!**"

"He's hysterical," Zola bit her claws. "Pythia's pants, he'll have every gorgon in the place after us."

"Sorry, Alf, it's for your own good!" Verity biffed him one in the chops and he fell over backwards.

Stunned into silence, Alfie blinked up at her with his wonky eyes. "Hey. You calmed me down with a boom!"

I would've groaned out loud but my teeth were too busy chattering in fear. Had the gorgons heard us? Zola and I joined Alfie and Verity beneath the overhanging rock.

"I don't understand," said Zola, staring out while her snakes looked at each other in confusion. "The gorgons . . . they're not moving?"

"Not one of them is looking our way," I said quietly. "In fact, their eyes are all closed!"

"They're . . . not doing anything much." Alfie got back to his feet. "Hey, you don't think they've turned themselves into stone, do you? That would be embarrassing!"

"No, they haven't." Verity pointed down into the valley, a look of awe on her hamstery face. "Look, where the water's falling on them – you can see . . ."

She trailed off. Perhaps because Alfie, Zola and I gave a synchronized gasp as we saw what her keen eyes had already picked out. On the back of each gorgon's head was something like a pink, pulsating veiny brain, clinging there with tendrils and tentacles. It was one of the grossest things I have ever seen (and if you've read this far, you already know the stiffness of the competition).

"Zooloobs," Verity whispered.

At first I thought she was swearing. Then I remembered. "Those things your uncle thought might be controlling me?" I shivered. "They're invisible till they're wet, isn't that what he said?"

"Correct," said Zola. "They normally float about down on the very lowest level, looking for victims. Once they've

stuck themselves onto the head of a monster, they push in their tentacles and feed on the brainpower. That means they can work their host's mind and body by remote control." She looked worried. "We used to get the odd one or two floating up from Level Seven, but never as many as this."

"It looks like they've overrun the whole place," I agreed, "and put the gorgons to sleep standing up. Maybe so they won't notice each other's zooloobs and kick up a fuss."

Verity nodded. "Ooooh, Bob-ob-ob, I bet you're right."

"Know what? I like zooloobs." Alfie grinned round at us. "Now we can whizz straight through this level and down to the Star Jewel without being noticed – am I right? Good old zooloobs. I love zooloobs! Mmm, y'know, I could probably marry a zooloob—"

"There's one floating up here now," said Zola.

"**AUUUUGHHHHHHHH!**"

Alfie jumped in the air, saw the horrible brain-thing bobbing up over the ledge through the dripping rain, its tentacles outstretched. But Zola pulled off her shades, fixed it with a gorgon glare, and – **WHOOSH!** – turned it into a bright red balloon. As it floated to the ground,

I jumped on the thing to pop it.

"Nasty, stinking zooloobs," Alfie muttered. "I've always hated them."

"Let's away to the helicopter and get going while we can!" Verity raised a paw heroically. "But remember, it's dry in here. We won't be able to see any zooloobs. Wave your arms in the air about your head just in case."

"Better still," said Zola with a smile, "my snakes shall perform a rich, historical tragedy entirely through the medium of mime, to distract any zooloobs from attacking us."

"By boring them to death?" said Verity, nodding. "Nice thinking, Zoles!"

I have to say, the sight of Zola's head snakes in their little hats and scarves, wriggling against a make-believe wind was strangely moving – it moved me all the way back to the copter at record speed, flapping my hands round my ears like an infant chased by a bee on a picnic. Alfie was pretty much the same, except with his small claw he couldn't quite reach his head. I was actually quite relieved to see that big old bum in the ceiling again, and our transport still parked beneath.

"All right, let's go." Alfie started up the engine as Verity and Zola bundled on board behind us and slammed the door. The gloopy rotors began to turn. "Which way now?"

Verity was already checking her notes. "Head south out of here. We have to follow the course of the River Plurge Rapids."

"Thank goodness we don't have to take a boat or swim for it." Zola patted her snakes' heads to stop their mime. They looked a bit disappointed (one rebelliously continued pretending to feel its way round an invisible wall). "Anyone who's ever tried to navigate the Plurge Rapids has been smashed into a billion pieces!"

"Nice," I said, as Zola's snakes mimed flopping down dead.

"Well, the rapids ought to lead us right down to Level Seven. And from there it's only a short hop over to our final destination: The Star Jewel!"

"Really?" Hope fluttered uncertainly in my heart, like a sparrow caught inside a shopping-centre piazza. "It's as easy as that?"

"Abso-bib-bobbb-ling-lootly!" Verity beamed. "Um, sort of."

My hope-sparrow whapped into a shopping-centre window and flopped down onto the litterbin of despair. "Sort of? What do you mean, sort of?"

"Well, Uncle says, before we can get at the crystal, we have to 'brave the lash of Old Mother Poison, the final guardian'. Whoever that is."

"Brave her lash?" Alfie's claws wobbled on the control stick as he nudged the copter forwards through the dark tunnels. "What, like, a whiplash?"

"Or maybe it's an eyelash?" said Verity. "Maybe she's just an old lady with a really long eyelash, and you have to sort of get past it without tripping up."

"Yeah, right," I sighed. "That's totally likely."

The copter soared out of the cave and into the rainy haze of morning. I gazed down at the sleeping gorgons and their zooloob horror-headwear, and half-wished I was oblivious to all that was going on around me.

"Cheer up, Bob-ob-ob. She'll be really, *really* old if she's been guarding it all this time." Verity nudged me with a furry elbow. "Hey, for all we know, she dropped dead a few centuries back. And even if the old broad is still clinging to life somehow – c'mon, we can take down an old lady, right? Four of us against one ancient old crone with a lousy whip?"

Reluctantly I considered the percentages, as usual. "I guess the odds are on our side."

"Right," Zola agreed. "So long as we don't fly into any rawks."

As one, Alfie, Verity and I turned to her and echoed: "Rawks?"

"Yes. Big birds made out of stone," she explained. "The rawks live among the gorgons because they're immune to our glares. You should see their poops! It's like showering in rubble."

"I think I'll pass," I said. "Are they friendly?"

"Oh, yes. Well, so long as you stay well away from them," said Zola. "No one tends to fly anywhere in Gorgonopolis, because at the first whisper of an engine in their air-space, they attack." Suddenly her snakes dived for cover, hiding their heads under their coiling, quivering bodies. "Like, um, those rawks heading for us now . . ."

I could already see them: a flock of misshapen, menacing gargoyles. The rawks numbered maybe twenty, with wings like gravestones, beaks like cones of concrete and glittering gravel for eyes. Veering towards us, they squawked loudly, a nerve-jangling sound like metal scraping granite.

"I'm guessing we're entering rawk air-space." Alfie had turned pale as the porridge stains on the windows. "Newsflash just in, guys — they're heading straight for us!"

CHAPTER 17

DOWN INTO THE RAPIDS OF DOOM

Before I could even draw breath to yell in super-scared fear, the rawks had descended on us. It was awful! The copter tumbled and pitched, as stony claws and concrete beaks swung and smashed at the windows. It was as if we'd been thrown into the 'concrete wash' in some insane sky-launderette.

"Lose altitude, Alfie!" Verity shouted, "Dip down to avoid them!"

Alfie pushed on the control stick, and we dropped — with a horrific shattering of rotors.

"Or not," Verity added quickly, "you decide!"

"We came down too fast," Zola said fearfully. "The rotors smashed into the rawks—"

"Yep, noticed, thanks!" Alfie was trying to steer, but the copter was swinging round, barely under control. "Now we're in trouble. This bird is falling!"

Spiralling below I saw a wide, frothing ribbon of water.

"Is that the river whatsitsname?"

"The River Plurge! Yes!" Verity nodded feverishly. "Head that way, Alfie. Head that way!"

"I can't! We're out of control," Alfie shouted. "We're going to crash!"

Down with the boom, I thought grimly. "If we hit at this speed, we'll all be killed. 100% certain!"

"No. There's a chance." Zola's claws were poised on her dark glasses. "I can use my gorgon glare on you – transform you into something that might survive the crash."

"Seriously?" I stared at her. "What about you?"

"Maybe if I look in the mirror, I can change myself too?"

BAM! I was thrown against Zola as one last rawk slammed into the side of the copter. Her shades fell free, and as Alfie turned round to her in wild panic –

SHMMMM!

One glance, and he was transformed into a bright yellow inflatable!

"Pilot down!" squeaked Verity, grappling with gravity and the blow-up Alfie as she took over the controls. "We've got to hit the river . . ."

"Verity, you could hardly steer a bus!" I reminded her,

panic stricken. "What makes you think you can handle a helicopter?"

"Dumbness and optimism," Verity admitted, as the copter jerked downward on its erratic course.

"At least Alfie will float." Zola considered. "I'm not sure about the colour though. Do you think the yellow's too bright—?"

"Just change us!" I begged her. "Quick!"

"I've never transformed a human before," Zola admitted. "Who knows what might happen?"

"Do it!" I pleaded. "It's got to be better than a mahoosive—"

WHAMMM!

Another rawk flew right into us, its white stony beak smashing through the window, sending us into a faster spin. *What if Alfie gets a puncture?* I thought.

Then I lost my grip on the seat and was thrown out through the broken window. And all I could think was, *NOOOOOOOO!*

"Bob-ob-ob!" Verity yelled. I saw her as if in slow motion, reaching out a paw to me. But it was too late. I was in freefall. Tumbling through the air like a skydiver, in a world where the sky was solid and the rivers would probably kill you with a single—

Ker-***SPLASHHH!***

I struck the surging white waters (I say 'waters' – who knew what it was) of the River Plurge. It was like landing on a slide in the wildest water park ever, only accelerated by around 92%. And 100% less fun. From the smell and thickness of the stuff I was now drowning in, it was clear that no chlorine had been close – it smelled more like raw sewage. I saw the copter, battered and dented and smashed, whistle and spin overhead like a trashcan comet, but the roar of its dying rotors was lost in the wash and bubble of the stinking rapids. The current was insanely strong. It sucked me under, sweeping me away.

"Ugh!" I spluttered. Where was the copter now? I saw something dark race by. A rock! I lunged for it, hoping to hang on – AAAAGH! The jagged edge almost sliced off my fingers. No traveller had ever survived this river, Zola had warned us, and now I could see just why . . .

I HATE THIS MONSTERLAND! I would've shouted if my mouth wasn't full of toxic sludge and if I wasn't exhausted already from fighting to stay afloat.

I SHOULDN'T BE HERE. I JUST WANT TO GET HOME!

Then, as I rounded a bend in the river, my sludge-splashed eyes widened. Hope flared somewhere inside. Because it occurred to me, perhaps those poor old travellers met their doom because they lacked a particular something.

They didn't have their own, bright yellow, Alfie-shaped inflatable to cling onto!

I saw the luminous lifesaver swoosh down the raging river towards me; Alfie must've been hurled from the copter too. But where was it now? I couldn't see anything in the sky besides rawks, raining their rubbly droppings over the river like a deadly hail. I ducked under the water again and was nearly sliced in two by a razor-sharp rock beneath the surface. When I broke the surface again I saw the Alfie-inflatable bearing down on me, and caught hold of his big claw. *WHOOOOOOSH!* Carried into an even faster current, we rocketed away.

Clinging to that buoyant claw, I could've wept for joy. I was so wet anyway, no one would've noticed. With a determination born of sudden, unlikely hope that I could survive, I clambered on top of the inflatable and clung on with frozen limbs. It meant that my face was pressed up against Alfie's butt, but he would never know and I wasn't planning on telling anybody (oops – keep it to yourselves).

Shivering cold, fighting to keep my grip as the water tossed us this way, that way, 7% further that way, back as much the other way –WHOAAA, how far THAT way did we go? Urghh . . .

How long did the River Plurge go on for? Did it ever end? Did it flow into some incredible subterranean sea, swirling ever deeper, round and round, until it fell boiling and steaming into the Earth's core?

I wished. That sounded like a walk in the park (or, perhaps, a soggy paddle in the lake) compared to the reality I saw stretching ahead in the distance.

Perhaps half-a-mile away there lay a churning, foaming mass of water and spray exploding over a fearsome array of jagged rocks, and beyond that . . . nothing. The world fell away, screaming.

It was a waterfall.

A water-heck-of-a-fall – but how far, and into what?

"Well. Guess this is goodbye." I knew then, this was it – the unhappy ending of my own Bob Bee B-movie.

Thanks a bunch, Fate! I thought bitterly. But I knew Fate couldn't hear a thing, too busy laughing her mystical stockings off at the idea that Bob, the boy who loved monster flicks above all else should meet his end in a land of monsters . . . trying to escape monsters . . . while floating on top of a monster . . .

Oh, and – by the looks of the dark, sinister lump catching up with me through the foaming rapids, ready to overtake – being EATEN by monsters too.

The sight left me stunned for a time. Then it made me angry. "It's not fair!" I shouted with the last of my strength. Didn't I have enough ways to die right now? I stared, appalled, as a macabre fish-creature reared up from the water, part-hammerhead-shark, part-octopus (I was too terrified to catalogue the exact percentages but at a guess I'd say about 32.7% fish, 67.3% eight-armed freaky-thing). Its six huge eyes were boggling laser-red, its tentacles snaked out towards me.

The nameless thing had the confidence and precision of a natural born predator.

I had the despairing shriek and highly wet pants of a living lunch.

I tore my eyes from its bulk, and yelped to find the line of rocky fangs at the waterfall's edge now horrifically close.

Looked back: the fish-thing was almost on top of me.

Looked back again: the rocks loomed larger still.

Looked back again, again: squiddy tentacles were closing on Alfie's bright yellow bulk—

Just as—with a *pffffft!*—Zola's gorgon transmogrification wore off. Alfie was back to normal! He was no longer an inflatable.

He was a sinkable.

"AUGHHH—BLUBBLEBLUBBLEBLUBBLE,"

Alfie managed as the two of us instantly plopped beneath the water — an escape manoeuvre which the fish-thing clearly hadn't expected. We plunged right through its tightening tentacles. As the current sucked us down I saw its bulky body speed overhead.

Now the creature was ahead of us! Alfie kicked with all his strength and together we bobbed up behind it — just as it smashed full-force into the rocks in a scene best put across in glorious picture-o-vision:

"*OOOOOOOGHHHHHH*," whaled the fish-monster ('wailed', I mean. Although, whales aren't fish, they're mammals, so the joke doesn't even work. Mind you, that fish-monster wasn't really a fish either. So maybe it does work? Get a pencil and correct it if you like, I won't mind.).

The stupefied beast clung on to the remains of the rocks for a second or two – until Alfie and I were swept into the back of it. **BLAPP!** Its squashy body saved us from death on the rocks and gave us a soft landing.

But our double-impact sent the monster-fish-thing flopping over the edge of the waterfall – into the stinging spray-storm of the abyss.

CHAPTER 18

BEWARE THE LASH OF FEAR OF MOTHER POISON (OF DOOM)

"WHOAAAAAAA!"

Alfie and I yelled.

Freefall! We tumbled through space, half deafened by the thunder of the falls. The air was so wet I could hardly breathe. Instinctively, I clung onto one of the fish-thing's fins (not exactly a teddy bear but all I had to hand); Alfie's pincers were clamped around it too.

FIN, I thought — they said that at the end of movies, sometimes: *FIN*, French for 'End', or 'Finish'.

And as Alfie and I went into freefall, 'FINISH' was

written large in my brain. Not 'finish' in Finnish – that would be, *LOPPU*. Which sounds like, 'le poo', which might be French for 'the poo', but which isn't: that would be, *le caca*. **Caca**n you believe it? Amazing what goes through your head when you're plunging to your doom . . .

The drop was so steep, it soon became clear that we weren't going to land any time soon. By clutching hold of the fish-thing (which was maintaining a dignified silence – either that or it was dead), at least Alfie and I stayed together as we fell. It made me feel a bit braver somehow.

"Alfie," I called to him over the roar of the falls, "you okay?"

"Er, not exactly!" Alfie called back. "I'm plummeting to my death!"

There was that, I suppose. "You know what I don't get?"

"Any good luck, ever?" Alfie suggested.

"Well, yeah. But I don't get why this thing attacked so close to the ledge. Or how it survives in such a deadly river."

"It's one tough-looking marine monster," Alfie declared. "I bet it's got a few tricks up its gills to help it—"

VRRRR-BOOOOOOSH!

Alfie and I yelled, thrown violently away from each other as the fish billowed outward. Suddenly its bulky body was wide and flat like a parachute, catching the updrafts, slowing its fall. Alfie and I just managed to hang on – and as we dangled there we burst out into wild whooping and joyous shrieks.

"So THAT's how it survives this river!" I laughed. "And how about that, so do— WHEEEEEEEEE!"

The thing shook us free with a casual shrug of its fins and started soaring back up the colossal falls. I hardly had time to hold my breath before I smacked down into the churning, stinking water. It was suddenly much warmer water too, almost like falling into a jacuzzi – a really stinky jacuzzi full of sewer waste. With the last of my strength I swam for my life . . .

And found the current washing me to the dark shallows at the side of the river. I spat out water and watched the flying fish-thing soaring back up the phenomenal falls, soon lost from sight in the haze.

"**WHOA!**" Alfie plopped up beside me. "We were very nearly *drown* with the boom, there!"

"Alfie," I panted, giving him a look, "could you please

think up another catchphrase?"

We both started to laugh. I tried to high-five him, and Alfie tried to high-five me back with his big claw. We missed, and that made us laugh harder. Given what we'd just come through, it was a nice feeling. It was nice to feel *anything*.

Slowly it sank in (the same way that I hadn't).

I was alive.

STILL ALIVE!

I'd like to say that after my dance with death (a rubbish, poorly-choreographed dance that even the kindest dance judges would give a minus-six) the world seemed brighter around me. But, no, it really didn't. It couldn't, really. Everything else around here seemed black — black cliffs, black sand, a black plain leading onto black dunes. Even the river, which ran calmer here, seemed black as it flowed away into a far-off, hazy horizon. It was like a seaside designed by goths.

"I wonder where the girls are?" said Alfie.

"Maybe Zola turned Verity into an inflatable and did the same for herself?" I suggested. "I hope so. Then maybe they'll wash up down here with us."

"Don't get your hopes up," said Alfie. "Most monsters hate doing the washing up."

I gave a little whimper. Not at the joke, which admittedly deserved one, but at the particularly black cave gaping right in front of me that had caught my attention. It was at least 5% darker than the other dark stuff all around.

"Think that's where the Star Jewel is?" I murmured.

"More than likely." Alfie nodded glumly. "It's the scariest-looking place around."

"Maybe you should check it out ahead of the others getting here," I suggested.

Alfie's wonky eyes narrowed. "Me?"

"You're scariest. You know—" I put my hands into claws and pulled my face into a pantomime grimace. "Grrrr, groar, I am Crudzilla!"

"Stop!" Alfie cringed. "It's too real, man! You're scaring me." He nodded to the cave. "See? You should go in. I'm just a comedian, you're the one with scare power. I mean, that toxic nose thing—"

"Enough of the nose!" I snapped. "Come on, Alfie, this is Monsterland! You're a monster, I'm not!"

"So, you have the element of surprise," Alfie countered.

WHO'S THERE? came a high-pitched, wavery voice from the cave.

I was so scared I jumped into Alfie's arms. Unfortunately, he was trying to jump into my arms at the same time. We collided and landed in a tangled heap in the black sand.

"Okay, fair play," Alfie whispered. "Whoever just said that has the element of surprise."

"Come in, if you're going to," came the voice again. "I'll put the kettle on for a nice cup of tea."

"Kettle?" Alfie looked blank. "Tea?"

"It's a human drink. My mum and dad like it." I looked at him. "The Star Jewel was made by a human called Merlin. I always thought he was made up, since the stories all said he was magic, but maybe that's him now?"

"Him?" The wavery voice sounded scandalised. "I'm a woman!"

"Um, sorry," I called back quickly. I peered into the cave, but it remained stubbornly dark. "Alfie . . . maybe we could both go in?"

"Okay," he said reluctantly. "That water was gross.

Maybe a cup of pee will take away the taste."

"Tea," I corrected him. "Unless it's camomile. Then you're bang on." Ignoring his confused face, I took him by the claw. "Here we go, then . . ."

We moved cautiously into the cave. As we did so, torches set into the rough stone walls burst into flame. And in the sputtering light, I could see the cave changing. The floor became wooden. The walls became smoother, painted white. Old furniture formed from the shadows, festooned with cobwebs like nightmare bunting. Grim-faced statues stood in strange, unnatural poses. A grandfather clock ticked heavily, like a slow heartbeat. There was a patch in the corner where the floorboards ran out, and crooked stones pushed up from soil like giant fangs. It was like standing in the hall of a haunted mansion. A rusty old-fashioned kettle was steaming over a small fire on the ground.

An emaciated old woman stepped forward to stand before us. *"Who are you?"*

I thought I'd be pleased to see another human being after all the weird monsters I'd witnessed down here. But I was wrong. The old woman's gaunt face and blue staring eyes were made all the spookier by the flickering torchlight shadows. She wore a dress embroidered with runic patterns that seemed to shift and shimmer in the half-light, as if the fabric itself was alive and trying to speak. She raised her arms and pointed her long talons at us, like a witch ready to cast a spell.

"Who are you?" she repeated. "Come on, the kettle's boiling."

"Um, I'm Bob," I said, accurately.

"And I'm Alfie Crudzilla," said Alfie. "How's it hanging, dude? Um, lady-dude."

But the old lady had closed her eyes as if concentrating. "A human child, here? Is this the time of prophecy?"

"Prophecy? I thought it was the time of cup-of-tea," joked Alfie nervously. "Boom! Yeah, I'm **DOWN** with the boom—"

"Silence, monster!" The old woman snapped. "Tea is for humans alone." She picked up the kettle and hobbled over to one of the tables. I saw two crude, clay mugs stood there, one clean, the other coated in dust and cobwebs. "Shall I be mother?" She smiled horribly. "MOTHER POISON, THAT IS!"

"For so long I have guarded this space," the old woman said. "Is it time at last for He Who Will Take Hold of the Star Jewel to claim his prize?"

"I'mmmm . . . not sure exactly what you're talking about," I admitted. "But I am looking for the Star Jewel, I need it to wish myself back home, you see, I shouldn't be here but my whole house was sucked in—"

"Silence, boy!" the hag squawked. "Try to trick me and it will be the worse for you."

A torch behind us suddenly went up like a roman candle; a fiery cascade of white sparks lit the room. Alfie and I turned to face a pile of misshapen skeletons stacked high against the wall. I clutched hold of Alfie and he pinched me with a pincer.

"You see, many have hoped to gain power over the Humamon Star Jewel," Mother Poison continued. "Many have broken in here, claiming to be the chosen one from above, the one of prophecy." She gestured to the skeletons. "You see what my lash did to them and their falsehoods." She paused. "Although, admittedly, one of them was just a tourist who'd lost his way and was asking for directions. Ooops. But, anyway!" She sipped her tea and gave me a leering smile. "If you are truly the chosen human and would hold the Star Jewel, you will have no problem telling me the password that will stop my lash…"

I swallowed hard. "Uh . . . excuse me?"

"The password that would have been handed down to you." Mother Poison smiled without humour. "You don't have it?"

"I bet Verity's got it," Alfie murmured.

"We'll have to wait till she gets here," I agreed.

"Oh, but by then the tea will be cold. I am ready to play NOW." She gave a toothless smile. "No trespassers may enter without feeling the lash of Mother Poison!"

"Look, lady," Alfie began, "why not forget all this weirdy-witch stuff and just let us through to the jewel thing?"

"Weirdy-witch? THAT'S IT!" Mother Poison pointed at Alfie. "You FOOOOOOL!"

There was a whip-crack sound –

wii-CHAA!

Alfie jerked his head as if slapped. "Huh? What hit me?"

"*I* did. Don't you know anything?" The old crone huffed. "You ID-EEEEEE-OT!"

The *wii-CHAA* sound cracked out again. "Ow!" Alfie's head jerked the other way.

"Now, show some respect," she snarled. "Monsters don't matter to me. But if you persist with such rudeness, I'll give you a *proper* tongue-lashing."

Alfie looked at me, incredulous. "That's 'the lash of Mother Poison'? A tongue lash?"

"Yes, a tongue lash!" She smiled. "What can I say? Poisonous words simply trip off my tongue, *you ridiculous, rubber-faced rat's bum!"*

"**ARRGH!**" With the sound of the whip-crack and a forked flash of lightning, Alfie was thrown back against the wall.

"What the . . .?" I raced over to Alfie to check he was all right, and he blinked up at me, dazed.

"I hope Verity makes it down here with the password soon," he said, weakly. "This old trout's pretty tough."

"Merlin would hardly have left me to guard his jewel if I wasn't." The hag pointed her fingers at me. "Password. Now."

"I told you," I said, "I don't know it! I didn't know I had to know it. My, um, guide has it, and she'll be along—"

"*Right now I'm trying to see things the way you do, sonny,*" she roared, "*but I can't get my head far enough up my butt!*"

The flash of lightning whipcracked around me. I was thrown backwards with a roar, banging into the bone-pile.

"Well, boy?" Mother Poison was looking at me, now. "You'll join those bones forever if you can't name me the word that will stop my lash."

"I keep telling you, I don't know it!" I cried.

The ghastly old bag tutted and shook her head. "*It looks like you fell out of the 'dumb-brain' tree and hit every single branch on the way down!*"

"Arrrrgh!" The whip-crack came again and I felt the power spark through my skeleton, jerking me out of the bone-pile and into a table. Pain seared through my brain. "Look," I gasped, "how would it be if my friend and I just waited outside?"

"No, no, no. You can't leave now. I've waited hundreds of years for a new victim to dress down." She sneered. "Though let me tell you, *talking to you is about as appealing as playing leapfrog with a unicorn!*"

Wii-CHAAA! Again the horrible power striped through me. I threw ridiculous shapes as I was propelled across the room. I throbbed all over. Barely conscious, unable to move, I saw Mother Poison float eerily towards me, eyes blazing.

"Dear, oh, dear," she sneered, standing over me. "One more blistering insult should finish you off for good."

Her mouth twisted open as she got ready to let rip with the final, killer line . . .

CHAPTER 19

THE INCREDIBLE APPEARING HOUSE OF MYSTERY

I turned away from Mother Poison's hideous grimace, braced myself for the next insult that would surely be the last I'd ever hear.

But then Alfie's voice rang out. "Hey, lady! You're not the only one who can trash-talk round here, y'know? I'm a stand-up comic. I know how to put down a heckler."

"WHAT?" I could see that Mother Poison's professional pride was hurt. She spun round and pointed at him. "You snivelling worm! *If you spoke your mind, you'd be speechless!*"

But before she could finish speaking, Alfie got his own line in: *"You're so ugly that when your dad dropped you at school he got fined for littering!"*

Wit-CHAAA! The lightning split *between* them.

Mother Poison squawked and Alfie gasped and both staggered backwards.

"You dare try to turn my tongue-lashing against me?" hissed the crone. "*You're about as useful as a vonky-donk on a mongoono-cycle!*"

I don't know what that means, and I may have misheard it – because again, before she could finish, Alfie shouted her down: "*Stow it, lady. If I wanted to hear from a bum, I'd fart!*"

Wiiiii-CHAAAAAI The whipcrack sound echoed round the cave, the lightning flashed again. Alfie got a jolt that shook him sideways, but this time Mother Poison was zapped to her bony knees.

"No!" she cried, sweat pooling in the deep lines of her face. "*You . . . you couldn't pour water out of a boot if the instructions were on the heel!*"

But the boot was well and truly on the other foot now, as Alfie took a stride towards her. "*Hey! Your face makes onions cry!*"

Wii-CHAAAAAI Mother Poison writhed in agony as the comic Crudzilla's tongue-lashing turned her own powers against her.

"*I love what you've done with your hair, Mother P – how'd you get it to come out of your nostrils like that?*"

Wit-CHAAAAA! The insult hit her hard, and with a cry and a clang, she went crashing into an old piano. The echoes rumbled round the cave for what seemed like minutes. I kept watching Mother Poison carefully, expecting her to rise to her feet and try again. But no.

"How about that, huh? I beat her! I won! I'm **DOWN WITH THE BOOOOOOOOM**, man!"

"You were awesome," I said truthfully. "And I guess we don't have to worry about a password any more. Let's see where this cave leads."

So we did. We walked on and on through the shadows, the torches on the wall flickering on as we passed. Motion-sensitive flaming torches? It sounded flaming ridiculous, but by now I'd learned not to question the weird stuff. It happened anyway.

And that was the understatement of the century as, after still more time spent walking, we reached a dead end that started to rumble and grate. It was as if the stone itself was straining to lay some kind of colossal egg: "**HNNGGGGGHHHHH!**"

A split appeared in the smooth dark stone, and soon it started to widen. I found myself gripping hold of Alfie's pincer, and he held my hand just as tight as we waited to see what fresh horror awaited us . . .

Imagine my face when I saw what awaited us was . . . the front door to my house.

MY HOUSE!

(Actually, seeing as I'm so generous, you don't have to imagine my face.)

The more the walls split open, the more of my house I saw, and the more I couldn't believe my eyes. So I gave my eyes a brief but brutal interrogation – and still I couldn't grasp it. The flaming torches and the candles seemed on my side, burning brighter, raising the levels of brilliance – although, frankly, things didn't get much more brilliant than this.

It was my house! I was 98.3% certain of it.

I recognised the scratch in the paintwork on the front door from where I'd fallen with the key the month before. I saw the chip in the windowsill from where I'd tried to climb inside the front room while dressed as a zombie two Halloweens ago. The cave roof somehow folded away into its own shadows, like an open-top car (or an open-top cave, anyway), and I could see the whole of my house – every brick still in place. There was my bedroom window, still ajar from where I'd fallen through it. There was the attic window and the roof, which from down here looked to be intact.

Did I mention IT WAS MY HOUSE??

"It's here," I breathed. "The weirdwind carried it down through all those levels and it's still in one piece!"

"That's kind of freaky." Alfie whistled. "I guess it's, like, Merlin magic, right?"

"I guess." I felt suddenly homesick – not sick of looking at my home, I mean sick of being down here away from everything I knew, feeling out of my depth (Merlin magic, for flip's sake!) and wishing I could get back.

Of course, to make that wish . . .

"The Humamon Star Jewel." I clapped Alfie on the arm. "Come on, it's got to be around here somewhere, right?"

"Maybe it's inside the house?" Alfie suggested, his different sized eyes taking in the brickwork. "Sure is different from the holes in the cliffsides back home. Want to give me the tour?"

I beamed. "Walk this way!"

"If I could walk that way, I'd be a human being instead of a monster."

"I wish!"

Alfie chuckled. "We'll both be wishing, dude – any moment now!"

The front door swung open as I pushed on it. I stepped into my hall and turned on the light. What a feeling! The coat-stand had fallen over and there were books and magazines all over the floor. But aside from the mess, everything looked okay.

I heard a quiet scuffling noise just behind me. Turning, I found Alfie scratching his head, looking all around. "You have, like, colour on the walls!"

"It's called paint. Zola's gonna love it!" I stuck my head in the downstairs loo. (Not literally. I mean I looked in through the door.) I caught movement in the water at the bottom; my reflection, of course. I'd half expected all the water to have drained away or soaked the carpet. But here it was, where it was supposed to be, just as I'd hoped.

Moving through to the living room, I saw furniture had crashed about and books and DVDs were scattered all over the place. But happily there was no sign of Rachel Thing squashed flat against the wall like roadkill.

I moved to the most important part of the room – the TV, which was lying on its back – and heaved it back upright on its stand. It was fine – not a crack, not a mark. I heard a quiet hissing noise. Coming from . . . the wall?

It stopped.

The pipes for the central heating, I thought. *And the hot water tank in the loft. What if they've leaked?*

"Wow, you have floors with fur on!" Alfie called from outside.

I joined him in the hall. "It's carpet."

"Wha—? You have a pet car?"

"Never mind." I turned and hurried up the stairs. The carpet was dry. Everything seemed just as I'd unwillingly left it, what felt like weeks ago. I caught a quiet pattering noise coming from my bedroom. Frowning, I threw open the door.

There was no movement except the curtain's flutter in the breeze (well, it was kind of an open-top cave now, right?), catching at the pages of my treasured *Monsters of the Movies* book that lay open on the sill.

I felt kind of emotional. I was back. Back in my own little world. My own little world, that was currently at the bottom of someone else's little world that was hidden beneath my wider, bigger world. And that Star Jewel was somewhere to be found around here – so soon everything would be back in its proper place, myself included.

I heard a pattering sound overhead. Or at least, I was 68% to 73% sure I did.

"ARRRRGH!" cried Alfie. "THERE'S

A FLAT FURRY MONSTER
IN HERE, STRANGLING
YOUR WASHBOWL!"

I ran outside, to find Alfie pointing an accusing pincer at the toilet mat on the bathroom floor. "Er, don't worry about that," I told him. "It's cool."

"What flattened him?"

"He never felt a thing, I promise." I listened out for the pattering noise, but I couldn't hear anything else. There was a funny smell, though. A kind of old, damp smell. Of course, it was most likely me and Alfie after our dip in the raging river water.

Alfie turned to me, looking a bit uncomfortable. "This house thing of yours is weird. But to you, everything's okay, right?"

"Right." I rubbed the back of my neck. "Except, Mother Poison didn't say anything about a house turning up behind her secret door, did she?"

"Well, she was too busy lashing." Alfie shrugged. "Maybe the crystal pulled your house right down on top of it?"

I frowned. "And squashed it, you mean?"

"Doubt that! The house passed straight through everything else without any problem, right?" He headed back to the stairs. "Maybe the crystal is on the other side of your house?"

"Out the back you mean?" I nodded thoughtfully, and led the way downstairs.

But I froze as I heard a bang. I hadn't imagined that. It sounded like the back door going. Cautiously, I crept down the stairs – ooh, yes, there was the creaky step, four from the bottom – this was really home! There were other quiet creaks and shiftings I couldn't place, but . . .

A squealing voice called from close by and almost stopped my heart: "**Bob-ob-ob? BOB-OB-OB!**"

"VERITY!" I jumped the rest of the stairs and dashed into the kitchen (which was covered in spilled cutlery, with the back door open). There she stood, outside, in an ice-blue cavern knee-high in dry ice, a bit like a film set. She made a bedraggled figure, fur and toga soaking wet – only her head was fluffy and dry. She glanced back, saw me, smiled with those big beavery teeth of hers, then stepped aside . . .

To reveal, rising up from the swirling mist, a

slender stone pedestal.

And resting on the pedestal, a many-sided gemstone, glittering like a star.

"Here it is, Bob-ob-ob." Verity's voice was hushed and reverent. "The Humamon Star Jewel." She danced about, threw back her head and whooped. "We've

ONLY GONE AND FOUND IT!"

CHAPTER 20

THE TERRIBLE NEWS OF SADNESS

There. It. Was.

"Whoaaaa!" Alfie came up behind me. "So that's it, huh? Are we **DOWN WITH THE BOOM** or what? Huh? Where's Zola?"

"Yeah." The spell of the moment was broken, and I looked around. "Where *is* Zola?"

"She . . . didn't make it." Verity looked at me solemnly. "The helicopter went out of control. I jumped clear before it crashed. But Zola?" She shrugged and shook her head. "Nahhhh. So, anyways! Come on, Bob-ob-ob. Jewel! There! Go get it!"

"Wait!" I was so shaken by the news of Zola, I had to sit down. To think that crazy-cool gorgon, so arty-farty, with her little dressed-up snakes, was now . . . No. I couldn't take it in. Not after all we'd been through together. "Are you sure she's . . . ? I mean, could you have—"

"Nope, no mistake. She's history. The copter crushed up when it crashed into rocks. Then it exploded. Then all the little bits exploded too."

Alfie slumped to the floor beside me. "That poor gorgon . . . she saved my life, man. Even if she trashed my copter." He sniffed. "It's so sad."

"I know." I was close to tears myself.

Remembering.

GORGON ZOLA, H.I.P. (HISS IN PEACE)

CHAPTER 21

THE GASP-MAKING REVELATION OF HORROR

"Er, Bob-ob-ob?" Verity waved from beside the pedestal. "Finished remembering, yet? Ready to get on?"

I glared over at Verity. "Zola saved our lives too. You don't seem very bothered."

"Oh, I am. Honest. It's very sad." Verity paused. "Still, at least Zola helped get us here, right? She didn't explode into fiery pieces in vain. Yay!" The hamster-thing took an impatient step towards me, and I saw a green glint in her eyes. "Now, come on, Bob-ob-ob! Crystal! Pick it up and wish yourself and your house back to the human world up above. What are you waiting for?"

"Um, you did say I could have a wish on that crystal too?" Alfie looked between us, awkwardly. "I mean, I'm stoked for you, Bob, man, even though I'm sad about the gorgon-dude, but . . . Well, I've got nothing left now, you know? No copter, no friends, my sisters are out to get me . . ."

"That . . . that's true." I wiped my nose. "Why don't you go get the jewel?"

"He can't," Verity snapped. "It won't work for monsters. Only humans."

Alfie blinked. "Huh?"

"Monsters can't even touch it." She crossed to the pedestal and reached for the jewel. Her paws went right through it, like it was a projection, some kind of special effect. "So, no wishes for monsters."

I could feel my frown getting deeper. "Well, I can wish for him."

"You can't," said Verity, "because the crystal will only grant your heart's desire. Someone else's doesn't count."

Alfie looked as devastated as a rubbery monster could. "You, uh, didn't mention this back when you wanted me to give you a ride, Vee."

"Didn't I? Must've slipped my mind." She tittered ditzily. "Sorrreeeeeeeeeee! Now, come on, Bob. Wish!"

"Wait!" I scratched my head. "I thought you came here

197

to take the crystal back to your uncle? How can you, if you can't even hold it?"

"Oh, no. I can't!" She sighed and blew a raspberry. "Silly old Uncle Voshto, not even knowing that. Still, he'll get over it."

"How did you know that when your uncle didn't?" I demanded.

"Er, lucky guess?" Verity giggled and nodded to the pedestal. "What are you waiting for, Bob-ob-ob?"

"For you to act normal!" I shot back. "Why are you being so weird?"

"*Because she's not who you think she is!*"

I gasped, and Alfie's jaw dropped as if on a hinge, as a green-tinged figure with a head full of snakes charged through the kitchen with one of Old Mother Poison's equally old mugs from the cave.

"Zola?" I gasped.

"Watch!" Zola, soggy and snarling and steaming mad, hurled the mug of water into Verity's face.

Verity squealed with surprise and dismay . . .

And then I did too, and Alfie joined me a nanosecond later.

Because, now Zola had made it wet, we could see something sitting like a horrible hat on that hamster-like head.

The bloated brain-body of a zooloob.

Verity was under its control!

"You snake-haired hag! I thought I'd got rid of you." The Zooloob throbbed repulsively, and the green in Verity's eyes deepened as she struck a savage fighting stance. "Well, I suppose I'll just have to finish you off myself."

"You're *not* yourself, Verity. That brain-thing is working you." Zola smiled grimly.

"And now I can see it, I can do something about it."

Quick as a flash, the gorgon whipped off her glasses and gave the zooloob her sternest glare. With a **PFFFT!** the thing on Verity's head froze and turned to polystyrene. Then – **WSHHH!** – it toppled from her head and landed lightly on the lino – where Zola stamped on it. With a nerve-scratching squeak it broke apart into bobbly pieces.

Zola replaced her shades. "I call this still life, *Sent Packing*!"

As the zooloob perished, Verity staggered. "I'm sorry, Zola!" she whispered, wide-eyed. "Sorry, everyone! I didn't . . . mean . . . to . . ."

Then her eyes flickered shut and she flopped forward onto her face, snoring noisily.

"Oh, Zola!" I ran up with Alfie and hugged her. "I was so scared you were dead."

"Well, dying can be pretty good for an artist's career," Zola considered. "But I'm not popping off just yet if I can help it." She looked down at Verity curled up on the floor. "After you and Alfie fell from the copter, spray from the rapids got inside. I saw the zooloob on her head. Before I could do anything she shoved me out and down I went into the waterfall."

"Whoa, man!" Alfie looked at her admiringly. "How did you survive that?"

"My snakes whirled around like a dozen little propellers," Zola revealed, "enough to break my fall without breaking anything else."

"But will Verity be okay now?" I crouched beside the twitching hamster-thing. "I suppose the zooloob must've got her in Gorgonopolis."

"No," Verity whispered weakly. "It found me on Level One. Ever since we met, Bob-ob-ob . . ."

I felt my eyes widen. "Since the beginning?"

"Zooloobs can't control humans, so it got to you through me . . . Made me fight Killgrotty . . ."

I stroked her wilting ear. "But, why did it want to help me?"

"It wanted to find the Star Jewel." Verity propped herself up on one paw. "It knew Uncle Voshto would never spill secrets to a stranger, so it made me go to him . . . and let Zola and Alfie come along because they could help us get down here in one piece."

Alfie eyed her suspiciously. "This is weird, man. You acted so normal."

"Except for when your eyes turned green," I remembered.

"That was the zooloob taking charge. The rest of the time it made me forget it was ever there," Verity explained. "I didn't know I was tricking you all."

"The Star Jewel doesn't work for monsters," I told Zola. "You can't make your wishes come true."

Zola's snakes jolted into the air in shock. Then they flopped down over her face in dismay. She parted her scaly fringe, gazing wistfully at the Star Jewel. "As all great artists say – 'oh, bum'."

"I'm down with the 'oh, bum'," Alfie agreed sadly.

I caught movement behind me and jumped. Someone was standing in the kitchen doorway. Someone I hadn't expected to see. She smiled at me.

"*Rachel?*" I saw Zola and Alfie huddle together, afraid, while Verity frowned. "It's all right, Rachel was babysitting when the house blew away."

"She sits on babies?" Verity stuck out her tongue. "You humans are weird."

Zola clutched her guts. "She's not going to fire toxic waste from her—?"

"No. Still no."

"I was looking after Bob when this dreadful thing happened," Rachel explained.

"I thought you fell out," I told her. "I thought I was all alone."

"No, Bob. I've been here all the time."

Alfie looked surprised. "We didn't see you when we looked round the house."

"Oh, I was here," Rachel assured him, with a smile. "I was asleep. I've been here such a long time. I didn't think you would ever come, Bob." She took a step towards me, and I thought I heard a quiet skittering noise from the floor beneath us. "Please, can you wish this house back to the human world now?"

"Yes . . ." I looked at the Star Jewel. "Since getting home

is my heart's desire, it's basically *all* I can do with this thing. So, why would a zooloob go to all this trouble just to help me leave?"

"Who cares?" Rachel shrugged and walked over to me. "Just say goodbye to these monsters and wish this house back to the human world."

"The human world?" I looked at her, feeling uneasy. "That would be 'our world'."

"Yes, of course. So, take us there."

I nodded, a horrible theory taking root in my thoughts. "I suppose you can't wait to get back on the phone to that rubber plant of yours."

"I miss my rubber plant," Rachel agreed.

"And your eight boyfriends need watering."

She nodded. "They'll be desperate for water."

"Do you think your humbugs will throw a welcome home party?"

"I expect so." The smile slipped from her face and her eyes hardened. "Do it, Bob. Do it now."

"You're not Rachel. You're not even human." I backed away. "Guys, she's something else. Something *pretending* to be Rachel!"

204

Quick as a flash, Zola whipped off her shades and glared at 'Rachel'.

But the impostor just laughed. "That might work on lesser monsters," she said, a low, unearthly note sounding in her voice, "but not on me."

Verity got up slowly from the ground, her voice a breathy squeak. "Who are you?"

"I am the horror that Merlin placed here so many millennia ago." 'Rachel' was glowing red now, her features shifting, blurring. I felt my sweaty skin crawl as her skinny form mutated into something huge and powerful – a mound of dark flesh, shining with veins, rippling with muscles. A face pushed out from the hunched shoulders – a mask of hate and brutality that sent goosebumps racing round my flesh – with three fierce shining slits for eyes and a jagged chasm for a mouth.

When she spoke again, it was in a low, groaning voice that chilled me to my toes. "Behold me! Banished from the world of humans . . . trapped in the foundations of Terra Monstra, still I am destined to rule over all.

I... AM... BOSSTRADAMUS!"

CHAPTER 22

THE TROJAN HOUSE

"It's her!" Verity washed her whiskers for comfort. "It was Bosstradamus controlling that zooloob!"

"I control them all," the monster bragged. "They have been my eyes and ears."

"And, er, your floaty brain things," Alfie added.

Bosstradamus nodded her revolting head. "Once I learned from Voshto the route you would take to reach here, I used the zooloobs to make the gorgons sleep – so you would escort Bob here without delay."

"You used us all." Zola put her dark glasses back on, perhaps to hide the fear in her eyes. "But the stories say Merlin buried you in a pit."

"I climbed out." Bosstradamus's revolting bulk quivered with monstrous laughter. "It took me fifteen hundred years . . . eating nothing but slime and rocks and mud to survive . . . but I climbed out. And found myself here, in the vault of the Star Jewel." She hissed. "How the mystical stench of that crystal taunted me in the depths of the pit ... how it teased and tantalised ... how I **HUNGERED** for its magical might."

Alfie turned to me and gulped. "Do you think she wanted it much?"

"But it was no use to you, monsters can't use it." I couldn't keep the shake from my voice. "So you needed a human to work it for you. You needed me. But that's not all, is it? You needed my house."

Verity, Alfie and Zola looked at me. "Your house?"

"It wasn't an accident, the way my whole house was pulled down here by the eerinium, was it?" I said boldly. "You used whatever weirdo powers you still have to make it happen!"

"So." Bosstradamus smiled nastily. "Bob has worked it out at last."

I turned from her, facing my friends. "The crystal grants my heart's desire, right? To put my house right back where it came from ... but, unknown to me, *with Bosstradamus hiding on board.*"

Verity squeaked. "Of course! She can hitch a lift inside

this house back to the human world."

"And pick up where she left off in Merlin and Arthur's time," I concluded. "Causing bother and evil and stuff."

"Bravo," Bosstradamus breathed.

"Well . . . you can forget it." I bunched my fists, swallowed hard and tried to act tough. "Cos, I – I'm not going to take you anywhere."

"Really?" Bosstradamus growled. "Then my friends and I had better come out."

Uh-oh, I thought. "Your . . . friends?"

"Listen!" Verity sniffed the air, pricked her ears.

The stealthy scrabbling noises I'd heard before had returned.

"Where are they coming from?" I hissed.

Zola pointed at the nearest wall, riveted.

"What is it?" Alfie twittered.

"I think . . . it's PAINT!" Zola gasped, and I groaned. "Bob, I am loving the paint on the walls!"

"I am not loving the creepy noises behind the paint on the walls." Verity was looking all about. The scratching, scurrying sounds were getting louder. My stomach lurched to see the walls around me were starting to bulge. The floor tiles were rippling. The ceiling was beginning to flake overhead as a scary scratching started up.

"I never planned to return to the world of humans alone, Bob," Bosstradamus rumbled. "I invited a few hundred evil close friends to join the party. Have you heard of the Trojan Horse*? I have created the Trojan *House!*"

CROOM! The kitchen walls burst open as creepy, scaly, utterly repulsive monsters came crawling into sight. Or oozing into sight. Or hobbling into sight. Or dragging themselves into sight by their eyeballs.

Zola pulled off her shades and glared hard at the horrific horde.

"Don't look at the gorgon!" Bosstradamus commanded, but too late for most, who were transformed into cardboard cutouts.

"Thanks, Zola," said Alfie bravely, whacking one two-dimensional monster away. "Now they're pushovers!"

Bosstradamus roared and made a grab for me – I just barely ducked in time. "Out of here!" I yelled, legging it past the sinister standees and out into the hall. But here too –

KRRRUMM! – revolting monsters were clawing their way through the floor and walls. A

*If you don't know the Greek myth of the Trojan Horse, look it up. Not NOW! What the flip are you like? This is the exciting bit!

swiping, nine-fingered claw sent me staggering back into the downstairs loo — where a glowing jellyfish with eyes was rising from the toilet bowl. Yelling with horror, I turned and saw more incredible monsters uncoiling and wriggling and squeezing out from the dark spaces beneath the living-room floor.

BRANNNG! The hall radiator was forced from the wall by the cackling monsters hiding behind it; the stupid thing smashed into my legs and sent me staggering into the dining room. Suddenly I was surrounded by evil-looking demons pounding their way through the plaster, ripping through the rug, reaching for me, clawing for me . . .

A two-headed monster lunged for my neck with clawed hands. I ducked and backed away, straight into some kind of revolting ant-creature with dripping, waxy skin . . .

It didn't move — and I realised that *all* the monsters around me had been turned into wax.

I looked up, in a state of shock, to find Zola in the dining-room doorway, dark glasses back in place but composure lost. The monsters in the hall behind her were standing still in leering, twisted aspects. "I don't know WHAT to call this still life."

"How about *Scared Stiff*?" said Alfie, trampling over the waxy mass of invading monsters and dragging me out.

The way through the front door was blocked by a towering, one-eyed yellow glob and a round orange thing covered in spikes. Verity whirled into action, high-kicking them out of the way, ninja-hamster style. "Oh my nibbly goodness," she panted. "These things are everywhere!"

"Too many," Zola groaned, as Alfie threw open the front door. "I can't transform them all."

The 'five-minute freeze' of Zola's glare had gone down to barely thirty seconds. The still lifes around us were already twitching back into their normal forms. Zola stared round at them all again, froze them back into place – but her snakes were looking sickly, and she had to lean against Alfie.

Next moment – **SPLAMMM!** – the kitchen door was pulverised as Bosstradamus smashed through it. Verity quickly shooed Alfie and Zola outside. But I lingered, transfixed with fear, in the doorway.

"If only you'd done as Verity or 'Rachel' asked you, boy, and simply wished us all away." Bosstradamus tutted sadly. "I would have killed you swiftly to say thank you – before slowly destroying every other human on Earth."

How sweet, I thought.

"But now, we'll have to do things the hard way." The three eyes of Bosstradamus blazed fierily. "There's nowhere to run, boy."

213

Obviously, I wasn't about to accept *that*. I fled after Alfie, Zola and Verity out into Mother Poison's cavern, leaving my shattered house and shattered dreams behind me.

"You *will* take us all to the human world, Bob!" Bosstradamus screamed after us. "By the time I've finished with you and your friends, you will be **BEGGING** me to let you take us . . ."

With a chill of despair, I knew she was right. Running would do no good. It would only delay the inevitable. We were outnumbered by several-hundred-to-four. We were stuck at the bottom of an underground Niagara with nowhere to run. And, weakened by her ordeals, it seemed Zola had already overstrained her snakes just by getting us out of the house.

"We're doomed," I panted.

"I'm bound with the doom," said Alfie (inevitably).

"Of course, you in particular, Bob, are extra-specially doomed," said Verity sadly. "And so is the entire human race. Doomed, doomed, doomed. Oh! Those poor little humans . . . Doomed!"

"Well, thanks for the pep talk." As we ran past, I noticed Mother Poison's body on the ground behind some crags. "In here," I hissed, "let's take cover. Alfie, maybe the old boot can help us."

"As a human shield?" Alfie suggested.

"Who is she?" wondered Verity.

I tried to shake Mother P awake — but she faded to smoking dust.

Verity gulped. "I mean, who was she?"

"Mother Poison," I said, my stomach turning. "I don't get it, she was breathing just now, how could she just disappear . . . ?"

"Forget it, man," said Alfie.

"It's all over," Zola said sadly. "Look!"

Peeping over the crags, I gazed back the way we'd come. I heard the scuffle and scrape of monstrous claws crossing the cavern and caught the ominous dance of shadows as Bosstradamus's forces approached.

"No." Verity put a paw on my shoulder. "She means, look the *other* way."

I did so — to find a soggy, sour-faced Captain Killgrotty and his greenie goon squad stamping into the cavern on their bundle of little legs. He looked madly angry.

Even so, hope leaped in my chest like an enthusiastic

but badly-coordinated goat. Here was a captain in the Monster Army, a creature who cared for the welfare of monsters. He'd want to sort out a situation like this, wouldn't he?

He pulled out the weird-looking goggly binoculars he'd used when he first met me and trained them on Verity. "The zooloob scanner shows she's clear," he snarled. Then his three eyes narrowed as they fixed on me. "**YOU ...**"

"Captain Killgrotty!" I fell to my knees and put my hands together, begging for mercy. "Please! Please, listen. There's about a million evil monsters chasing after us, and they're led by—"

"Bosstradamus." His snarl bulldozered over my words. "I know. Who'd you think I was talking to, dangling beneath your copter? 'You'll bring disaster down on us all,' I said. 'You landed yourself here, and you'll never get out,' I said. 'Let the fluff-ball go,' I said."

I gulped. "Um, I thought you were talking to me."

Killgrotty waved his weird binoculars. "I knew that fur-brained Verity was being controlled by a zooloob. And I knew Bosstradamus would be behind it. I knew she was trying to lure you down here to use the Star Jewel for her mad, evil schemes." He glared at Alfie. "So, before you shook me loose,

I stuck a bug on your copter."

Alfie stiffened. "That's cruelty to bugs, man."

"A tracer, I mean, so I could follow you wherever you went." Killgrotty smiled grimly at his bedraggled guards. "And that's just what we've done, right, boys? All the way here."

His guards grumbled and nodded.

I could hear the clawing, slopping, clopping clatter of monster paws and feet coming closer – the sound of Bosstradamus's forces, recovered and in pursuit. "So you'll stop her, then?" I pleaded. "You'll stop Bosstradamus destroying the human world?"

"Sure, I will. There's one very simple way of stopping her. By eliminating the one person who can work that stupid Star Jewel . . ." Killgrotty pulled out his gun and aimed it straight at me. "By eliminating **YOU**."

CHAPTER 23

THE STARE OF CERTAIN DOOM

"Um . . ." I stared down the barrel of Killgrotty's gun. "When I asked for help, this isn't quite what I had in mind."

"You can't do it!" Verity squealed, and threw herself at Killgrotty. But his guards grabbed her, held her back. Zola tried to glare at Killgrotty, but another guard gripped her head-snakes in his big green hand and squeezed, forcing her to her knees.

"Leave us alone, man!" Alfie whumped the guard with his big pincer, but another greenie took his little claw and twisted hard. Alfie was out of action.

"That's enough, small-fry," Killgrotty snapped. "We have to do this. With human-boy out of the way, Bosstradamus and her rabble have no way out. There's nothing they can do."

"Er . . ." Verity gulped and pointed with her nose. "Did you tell them that?"

218

I peered out from behind the crags to see a seething, surging mass of creatures crawling and pouring from the cavern shadows. My heart pounded like Frankenstein's monster falling down a flight of stairs. I turned away, and found the gun-barrel jammed up against my nose.

The cold metal tickled my nostrils.

And suddenly – I *SNEEZED*.

AAAAAH-CHOOOOOOOO OOOOOOOO!

"AAAAUGHHHHHH!"

Killgrotty's guards shrieked and jumped backwards.

Verity was free again. She winked at me and hollered,

"TOXIC WAAAAASTE!"

"YIIIIIIIIIIII!" Alfie pretended he'd been hit in the eye and fell forward. "It burns! **OW! OWWW!** Nooooooo…"

Killgrotty stared at me, wide-eyed with fear. Going

cross-eyed, I realised a couple of gloopy snot-strands were hanging from my nostrils.

And it seemed Killgrotty's greenies were no match for mine. "**EEEK!**" wailed the guard holding Zola, bursting into tears. Another of Killgrotty's gang wet his pants. Yet another wet the pants of another guard standing several metres away.

I would have cheered, but, unbidden, another sneeze was coming — a real, riotous roar of one.

"YAAAAA-CHOOOOOOO!"

I aimed this one at the heaving horde of horrors charging our way. It froze those at the front of the pack almost as well as Zola's gorgon-glare — which meant they were quickly trampled by the monsters coming up behind, who couldn't stop in time.

Keen to cash in on my success, I faked another couple of noisy sneezes — though I well knew from monster movies that sequels were rarely as good as the originals. Even so, a lot of Bosstradamus's monsters cringed and backed away, while one of Killgrotty's guards turned and bolted. In fact, he led a minor charge, as the rest of the greenies legged it after him.

"Come back, you scum!" Killgrotty bawled after them.

And while he was distracted, Zola's head snakes lashed out and bit his wrist. "Ow!" he yelped, and dropped the gun. Verity caught it neatly, rolled over behind the crags, then jumped in and out of cover, firing blasts of red energy into the oncoming swarm of monsters. They hopped and dodged and dived for cover, as the sizzling splats of energy zwooshed about them.

"Oi! Not so fast!" Killgrotty snarled, lunging for the weapon.

As he did so, Alfie grabbed hold of his neck with his little pincer. I winced – what chance did he have? Except Killgrotty suddenly collapsed, slumping groggily to his knees, his eyes flickering shut.

"Squeezed his bethemma nerve," Alfie explained happily. "A delicate touch is all you need for a knockout."

"And a blaster!" Verity squealed, zapping blast after

blast into the scattering monster crowd.

We're going to win, I found myself thinking. *We're actually going to make it out of this!*

"No," Killgrotty grunted. "I meant . . . don't *fire* so fast . . . Power almost . . . out . . ."

And then so was he, already snoring as he struck the ground.

Zola, Alfie and I turned to Verity. "Stop!" we hissed, trying to grab the gun off her. "Stop firing!"

"Huh? When I've got them on the run?" She fired one more blast – but the sizzle had become a fizzle that could hardly zap a mouse, let alone a monster. "Uh-oh."

Zola raised her head over the crags. "Er, let that be a lesson to you!" she yelled at the crowding creeps. "Kindly go home." Then she lowered her voice. "Do you think they'll listen?"

"DON'T BE TAKEN IN BY THESE DESPERATE FOOLS!" Bosstradamus herself had lumbered outside on her thick, veiny legs, swinging her brutish face this way and that. "THEY CANNOT HURT YOU".

Alfie winced. "I don't think they're going to listen to you, Zoles."

"Maybe this'll shake them up," I murmured, and jumped up into sight.

"AAA-CHOOOO!"

I bellowed, as explosively as I could.

Many of the monsters recoiled, but Bosstradamus only sneered. "He cannot harm you," she told her followers. "That is simply a sneeze... The human equivalent of a friction gloop."

"**Ohhhhhhhh!**" came a great murmur of understanding from her murderous monsters – one that was shared by Zola, Alfie and Verity.

"I did wonder whether it might be a friction gloop," Alfie admitted.

"Shut up!" I hissed. "Bosstradamus just gave away that I'm harmless, our only gun has run out of power, Killgrotty's out cold and his greenies have scattered. What can we do?"

Alfie considered. "Cry and then soil ourselves?"

"**ALL RIGHT!**" Bosstradamus rasped. "You know there's no way out, boy. Say goodbye to your pathetic little pals, and then come out here and face your destiny."

"If I do," I called, "will you let Verity, Alfie and Zola go?"

"Um, yes. Of course." Bosstradamus sniggered. "I definitely won't stomp them into mush and feed them to my army before we leave."

Alfie slapped both pincers to his forehead. "She's totally going to stomp us into mush and feed us to her army before she leaves, isn't she?"

"Uh-huh," chorused Zola and Verity.

"Could you maybe give me five or six hours for the goodbye part?" I called again.

"You've got two minutes," Bosstradamus shot back. "Delay any longer and your friends will suffer **TERRIBLY**."

"As an artist, I rather hoped I'd be famous in my own lifetime." Zola was close to tears. "But since I don't have enough stare power to stop all those monsters . . ."

"There's only one thing for it." Verity looked sadly at Zola. "If this is the end . . . can you turn us all into something that won't feel pain?"

"No!" I felt my throat tighten. "It can't finish like this."

"Well, for you, it won't, man!" Alfie forced a cheery tone. "You'll be kept alive long enough to take Bosstradamus and her hordes into your world so they can run amok and destroy millions of humans in a futile act of revenge against a long-dead wizard."

"Oh, yeah, right. So it's not all bad then." I gave Zola an encouraging smile. "Can't you turn us into balloons so we float out of here and take you with us?"

"My creative batteries are drained." Zola batted a limp-headed snake. "I don't know how long you'd stay transformed, but it wouldn't be long enough to get back up the waterfall."

Verity washed her paws anxiously. "And even if we did, we'd just be washed straight down again."

"And besides, I've told you," Zola went on, "I've never transformed a human before. Who knows what might happen?"

"But there's got to be *something* we can do," I insisted. "I've seen so many monster movies where the good guys were holed up someplace, surrounded by creepy critters. No matter how tight the scrape, however terrible the villains, in around 94% of cases they get out in the end."

"This isn't a movie, man," Alfie reminded me.

"I wish it was," squeaked Verity.

"Perhaps it can be. Sort of." I looked at Zola. "You're an amazing artist. Can't you imagine really terrifying monsters — scary enough to scatter that army?"

"**Scary**," came an echo on the air. It sounded like Mother Poison but, no, she was only dust now. I had to concentrate on what was real: like, the deadly danger we were in.

"Good idea, Bob-ob-ob," said Verity. "Zola could work us like puppets! Super-creepy monsters like the Chopper and the Crudzilla sisters—"

"And Killgrotty," Alfie added.

"And the bouncer at The Severed Arm," I added some more, "all mixed together. The scariest bits of each, to make the scariest monster anyone's ever seen!"

"*Seen*," the strange voice whispered again. There was a lower note in it this time, like a chorus. "*Seen*." I peeked over the crag to make sure nothing horrid was sneaking up on us. But the pack of monsters was still waiting across the cave with Bosstradamus.

"One minute left," snarled the monster mastermind.

"Do you think you can do it, Zola?" Verity wondered. "Freeze us into monsters that'll give this bunch the willies and wave us around a bit to scare them away?"

"I have only limited experience of the art of puppetry," said Zola bravely, "but I'll try to work you all alone."

"*You all alone*," came the echo in my ears – no. In my

226

MIND. I felt dizzy. "You all alone," the voices were telling me.

"Me," I said quietly. "Use all your energy, Zola, the last of your powers to turn ME into a thing that'd give any monster in the world nightmares for months, just by looking at it."

Alfie looked worried. "You?"

"If I'm a monster, I can't use the crystal," I reminded them. "The longer I stay that way the better. And the bigger and nastier Zola can make me, the longer the rest of you will have to run for it. Maybe you'll find another way out."

Zola looked flustered. "I told you, I've never changed a human before now!"

"Try," I urged Zola. "You have to try. I've been sent behind the sofa by scary monsters in my time . . . maybe this lot will run off too."

Verity looked doubtful. Alfie looked doubtful. But Zola was smiling, even as little tears rolled down her green gorgon cheeks.

"I'll do my best," she promised. Then she lowered her head and pulled off her dark glasses, letting them slip to the ground. "Let's all hold hands and stand in a circle. Share and focus our energy. It's worth a try."

"Abso-nibblin'-lootly," said Verity, thrusting one paw into my hand, and one into Zola's.

"I never held hands with a lady-dude before." Self-consciously, Alfie gave his big pincer to Zola, and his little one to me.

"THIRTY SECONDS!" bellowed Bosstradamus.

"Try to relax, Bob," Zola said. "Clear your mind, like an artist about to start a brand new creation. Don't think about all the monsters behind you."

"All the monsters," came the echo again. The low part of the voice was stronger now; a man's voice, cracked with age. "All the monsters." He sounded urgent, insistent. "All the monsters . . ."

"I'm ready, Zola," I whispered. "GO!"

CHAPTER 24

MONSTER SMASH

Zola raised her head and fixed me with her eyes. I gasped as my body seemed to take root, fixing me to the ground. Amazing colours swept and sparked through Zola's irises as they grew larger, darker. Her snakes were waving and coiling as if conducting an orchestra of unknowable forces all about me.

I found I couldn't look away.

("All the monsters!" came the voice. "Scary! Think!")

My bones felt stiff, my skin was burning.

("You alone! All scary!")

I was so scared in any case that it was hard to summon up much in the way of new terror. And the words I'd heard, they were shifting, sifting through my head, finding new patterns...

("You – alone for now – think scary! Be all the monsters...")

My brain felt like it would squelch out black goo like the ghastly monsters in *Fiend Without a Face*. Oh! Those horrid brain-things, even creepier than a zooloob... It made me realise that the monster-mash in Zola's mind might be scary, sure – but those things would be KNOWN to Bosstradamus and her scumball army. If only I could show her the monsters from all the old movies I'd watched, over and over on so many late nights and lazy afternoons.

Suddenly, all that watching felt almost like TRAINING.

That was a scary thought.

"THINK SCARY!" the voice bellowed in my mind.

And so I did. As I stared into Zola's swirling eyes, I started to piece together the perfect scary monster in my head – a masterful mash-up of all the creepiest, craziest critters ever to make it to screen. And this wasn't some slapdash creation. Oh, no.

Because as usual, I was using percentages.

I'd make it 20% King Kong, giant-sized, hairy and tough . . . 22% The Blob, squelching and sucking up all who come near. 6% Dracula, for fangtastic chills . . . 10% Creature From the Black Lagoon, cos it's so flippin' creepy . . . 24% DinoBeast, tipping the scales with jaws and claws and a terrible tail. 12% bug-eyed mutant monster from this one movie I saw in glorious, goriest Technicolor, because that thing was just sooo weird . . .

And while my body began to transform, I held the mental image of my monster-mash-up in my mind. I felt jelly flesh squeeze through my human skin . . . the crack of my spine as my body turned scaly, hunching over. Strength hummed through me; with Zola's eyes on mine, I had never felt so powerful . . .

I remembered what she'd said about turning her gorgon glare on me, back when we were trudging towards the Wilderness Forest: *"Your body make-up is so different to a monster's. Can you imagine what might happen?"*

Well, I have plenty of imagination. And I imagined myself not a still life like Zola's other creations – but a *full-of-life*.

"Whoa, man!" I heard Alfie cry. "He's moving! *Bob's still moving!*"

In fact my whole body felt zinging with movement, as my artistic creation came cartwheeling into life! My jaws were getting longer. I was building massive muscles. I was growing so much larger, so much tougher and taller, stranger and crazier – but I could control my new body well, because my percentage fixation had left *all* my body parts in perfect proportion!

How long did I have in this incredible form? I didn't know. But I saw Zola fall to the floor, saw Alfie and Verity dragging her away, and knew that now – right now – success or failure would be down to me.

I stared at the assembled monster masses below – they looked so small, suddenly, like ants beneath my feet – and I bellowed down at them at the top of my King Kong lungs:

"ROOOAAAAAAAAAAAAR!"

And at once, those masses scattered.

"Cowards!" Bosstradamus hollered. "Come back! Come back, you—"

I guess my nemesis never knew what hit her – but for the record, it was a double-whammy of DinoBeast claw and King Kong foot.

"Groooooohhhh!" She went flying through the air and smashed into the cave wall. **WHUMPH!** The impact knocked a crater in the rock, and even from my great, enormous height I'm sure I could see little tweety-birds flying round her dazed head.

Suddenly I wasn't a victim any more. Suddenly, I was fighting back. And as the realisation struck me it felt as strong and intoxicating as the power Zola had poured into me.

I felt prickles and scratches at my legs. Some more marauding monsters were attacking, trying to bring me down. I barely felt their blows, but decided it would be rude to ignore them. I leaned over and bellowed, blowing several away. Then I brought down my big Blob fist on the ones still left. The hapless monsters were squelched and sucked up and absorbed with horrible speed – just as I'd always imagined the real Blob would do.

I stomped about, waving and boggling. Since my face resembled a hideous Hollywood fiend, with King Kong's hair and Dracula's fangs and an extra-large mutant brain-case, it's fair to say that Bosstradamus's gang had never seen a more far-out and frightening creation.

I heard Alfie's voice far below. "See that? **ALL HUMANS CAN DO THAT!**"

"It's true! Every single one of them can," Verity added in an authoritative squeak. "The toxic-waste nose thing was just a joke, but THIS is what they do when they're mad . . ."

"It's lies!" Bosstradamus wailed, watching what was left of her army fleeing the scene at high speed. "Lies! We can conquer the world . . . destroy all humans . . ."

"I don't think so, Bossy-boots!" Zola cried, getting

uncertainly to her feet. "You're the pits . . . and that's where you belong. Right, Bob?"

"**RAWRRRRRRR!**" I agreed, and stretched out a King Kong paw to gather up Bosstradamus. She struggled and twisted in my grip, but she couldn't get free. I strode right over my house, stepped over the Star Jewel on its pedestal and, in the sudden darkness beyond, breathed DinoBeast fire to light my way. There was a great, jagged split in the ancient rock. The pit into which Merlin had cast Bosstradamus, so long ago.

"It took you fifteen hundred years to climb out?" I hissed through Dracula's creepy vocal chords. "Well, don't worry. It's a much shorter journey going **DOWN** . . ."

I raised Bosstradamus, struggling, high into the air – then hurled her down into the pit with all the strength I could muster.

"**NOOOOOOOOOOOOOO!**" she screamed, hurtling from sight into the shadows of the pit. Her cries echoed around the ancient rock for almost a minute.

Then the echoes, like Bosstradamus, were gone.

CHAPTER 25

THE END?

There was a loud **PHFFFT!** in my head, and suddenly I found myself back beside the Star Jewel on its pedestal. I had regained my Bobness! I was back to normal size, normal body and, well . . . just normal.

Zola's glare had completely worn off, and for a moment, terror seized me – a rehearsal, so I imagined, for some disgusting monster grabbing me just as sharply. But, no. There were no other monsters around. No others, besides—

"Verity! Alfie! Zola!" I held out my arms to my fabulous friends, and they bundled over, wrapping me up in a hug. "Zola, whatever you did—"

"Wasn't I AMAZING!" Zola cried. "As artistic statements go, that was . . . well, it was . . ."

Verity squeaked. "It was 'boom'!"

"It was **DOWN WITH THE BOOM, MAAAAAN!**" Alfie picked me up and squeezed me happily. "How much do you rock, Bob? Thanks to Zola you trashed, like, the whole army and threw Bosstradamus down to the bottom of the world. We've got at least another fifteen hundred years till she can climb out again!"

"You," said Killgrotty, who was wide awake now, and staring at me in wonder. "You . . . the four of you, you . . ."

Verity smiled at him sweetly. "We rock?"

"We kick butt?" Zola suggested.

"We're down with the boom?" said Alfie.

"You're . . . **UNDER ARREST!**" Killgrotty's face had darkened. "Under arrest for... well, I mean, for almost

EVERYTHING IN THE WORLD!"

"Uh-oh." I turned to the Star Jewel beside me and picked it up from its pedestal. At once it glowed pinky-orange in my palms. "I think this thing is switched on," I told Killgrotty with a smile that was leaving 'mischievous' behind and moving on to 'wicked'. "And you know what? I really wish that you and your greenie gang were a long way away . . ."

"What?" Killgrotty's three eyes were twitching with rage.

"PUT THAT THING DOWN IMMEDIAT-"

Too late. Suddenly, he was gone.

"Woo-hoo!" Verity hitched up her toga and did a little dance. "Wishes come true! How about that? The Star Jewel works!"

"I'd like to try another test." I turned back to my trashed house – an unholy (or rather, very holey) mess of broken walls, smashed ceilings and splintered floorboards. "I wish my house was all fixed up and like it was before Bosstradamus got her paws on it!"

A blur of uncertain colour engulfed the house and then, **POW!** There was my house, back to how it was, all fixed up in a flash.

"You have but one wish left," came the stern, male voice I'd heard in my head before. "Use it wisely, Robert Bee ..."

Verity, Zola and Archie were looking round, trying to locate the source of the voice. I pointed to the dust that Mother Poison had left behind when she'd disappeared. Now it was spiralling up from the ground and a very different figure was forming and transforming . . . a tall, skinny man in a pointed hat, with long grey hair and an extra-bushy beard. He wore a long cowl, covered in the same runic symbols as Mother Poison. He looked at me, his eyes dancing with power.

"Who's this cranky-looking old dude?" Alfie said.

"How dare you!" the old figure grumbled. "I am the wizard Merlin."

"Merlin!" Verity gasped. "The founder of our world."

"Amongst other things," Merlin agreed grandly.

I was feeling a bit 'euwww'. "Er, did you just form out of Mother Poison's leftovers?"

"They were my own leftovers, thank you very much!" Merlin looked at me with disapproval. "When I first created Terra Monstra, I appointed Mother Poison to guard the Star Jewel – and so used my magic to extend her life by hundreds and hundreds of years. That magic bond was like a thread running from this world to mine, it left me linked to her, you see? So I could look in on the old place from time to time."

"As you do," I murmured, slightly blown away by all

I was hearing. (I mean, MERLIN?)

"Now the danger has passed and the Star Jewel no longer at risk," the old wizard continued, "I have released Mother Poison from her long, faithful service."

"By turning her to dust? Harsh, man." Alfie shook his head. "Couldn't you just have given her a gold watch or something?"

"I have returned her to my own time and place, in Camelot, just as young and pretty as once she was." Merlin paused. "Which wasn't really very young and pretty at all. But then, an old duffer like me can't be too choosy." He waved dismissively. "Anyway, think not sadly of her, but joyfully of me! For I planned for this moment, long ago and it's worked! I foretold everything, you see."

"Everything?" Verity echoed.

"EVERYTHING!" Merlin was practically dancing from foot to foot in excitement. "I foresaw that Bosstradamus would one day rise from the pit in which I'd left her ... that the unavoidable leaking of eerinium would affect matter in the immediate area above ground . . ."

"Wow," I breathed. "And you even saw that I would end up here?"

"Of course!" Merlin boomed. "Well, I predicted it would be you or someone in your family. Or if worse came to worst, a family pet. Oh, and be oddly obsessed with percentages too." Merlin looked a little uncomfortable. "Basically, Master Bee, I ensured that most of those who lived in your home would love monster movies, and so grow well-versed in monster lore and legend, the better to become my multi-monstrous champion in the final battle I saw coming."

"Wow," I frowned. "I feel so special."

Merlin moved on quickly. "I, er, even foretold that these brave, proud monsters here would find you and lend their skills to your struggle . . . And that one would betray the others, through no fault of her own." He gave Verity a sympathetic smile. "And rather cleverly, I allowed for it all! I knew that Bosstradamus would one day seek to draw Bob's house here . . . and that she would summon the most evil monsters in this land to hide inside it." He tapped his long nose. "And I decided that this was the perfect moment to strike back."

"Because all the evil monsters were in one spot – ready to be dealt with once and for all!" Zola's snakes looked at each other, impressed. "Nice foretelling!"

Merlin looked very smug. "Wasn't it just?"

"Except, I didn't know the password to get the crystal," I pointed out. "And so your servant, Old Mother Bag-Face, nearly totally killed me."

"Er, really?" Merlin looked a bit shifty. "I must have overlooked that!"

"Actually, *I* had the password." Verity started searching her pockets. "It was in Uncle Voshto's notes."

"I knew it!" Alfie sighed.

Verity handed me some paper. "Look, there it is."

I squinted at the page. "Then . . . the password was 'omma-chonga-nunga-phrrrr'?"

"Oops." Merlin started playing with his beard. "That's actually the old password, anyway. I changed it

I frowned. "Huh? Do what Bosstradamus wanted to do, you mean?"

"Yep! Only without the mass destruction part. Think about it." Verity put her paws around Zola and Alfie. "You want to be a stand-up comedian, Alf? Humans **LOVE** comedy. They have **LOADS** of comedy clubs. They'll love you!"

"They will?" A smile spread slowly over Alfie's face. "Hmm . . . yeah, maybe they will!"

"But he looks like a boy wearing a monster-suit!" I protested.

"So?" said Verity. "That's his gimmick! Now, as for you, Zola, you want to be a proper artist with your own studio."

"But no one appreciates my talents round here," Zola sighed.

"Well, then, be an artist in the human world! They have TONS of weird and crazy and incredibly expensive art that clever people buy and pretend to like, when really they don't understand it at all."

"Really? This sounds HEAVENLY!" Zola beamed at me. "Oh, yes, Bob, I am coming with you for certain."

Alfie nodded. "Me too, man!"

"You are?" I smiled wearily. "Well, I guess maybe you could stay in the cellar, at the very bottom of the house."

"Oooh, yes!" Zola clapped her pale-green hands. "And from there, if we ever get homesick, we can sneak down through the crack in the ground that started this whole business and visit Terra Monstra!"

I looked at Verity. "And what about you? Will you come?"

"Ooh." She looked at me warily, nose twitching. "Would . . . would you like me to, Bob-ob-ob?"

I thought. And then I grinned. And then I said, "ABSO-NIBBLIN'-LOOTLY!"

"Wheeeeeeeee!" Verity jumped into my arms and we hugged each other tight. "I've studied human beings through humanoscopes for so long, Bob-ob-ob . . . it'll be AMAZING to study them in the flesh! Just think! I'll dress up and disguise myself in your old clothes and watch hundreds of humans going about their daily business: working, playing, going to the toilet . . ."

"You will NOT watch them going to the toilet!" I insisted.

"Well, maybe not all the time." She hurried into the kitchen. "Come on, guys! Let's go. Another life begins today!"

"How about that?" Alfie clapped a friendly claw on my shoulder, then ambled after her. "I guess it does."

"It does, it does for sure." Zola ran inside with him, gazing with wonder at the kitchen cupboards and the walls. "Ooooh, I still can't believe it. Actual paint! Paint, all over! Oooooh . . ."

I watched Verity lead Alfie and Zola through to the hall, chattering excitedly. Then I turned to the crystal. I hesitated.

Was this wise, I wondered? Going back to my ordinary life with three crazy monsters in tow? Taking a piece of tricksy Terra Monstra back up above with me – how was that a recipe for trouble-free living?

Then I smiled. Who wants an ordinary life, anyway?

I made my wish, touched the Star Jewel and then hurried into my house.

The choice was made. The whole house trembled, shining with light. The gloom outside was fading, becoming bright with colour. Already I could see trees starting to form outside, and tarmac and streetlamps and parked cars and other houses and all that wonderful normal-world stuff I thought I'd never see again.

I was going back home and, yes, Verity, Alfie and Zola were coming with me.

Of course, I knew I couldn't have stopped them even if I'd tried . . .

How could anybody stop those monsters?